*A
Harlequin
Romance*

THE YEAR AT YATTABILLA

by

AMANDA DOYLE

HARLEQUIN BOOKS

Winnipeg • Canada   New York • New York

THE YEAR AT YATTABILLA

First published in 1970 by Mills & Boon Limited,
17 - 19 Foley Street, London, England.

Harlequin Canadian edition published November, 1970
Harlequin U.S. edition published February, 1971

The Harlequin trade mark, consisting of the word HARLEQUIN® and the portrayal of a Harlequin, is registered in the United States Patent Office and in the Canada Trade Marks Office.

Standard Book Number: 373-51448-4.

Printed in Canada

CHAPTER ONE

MADDIE MASTERTON looked at the face of the man sitting in the chair adjacent to hers in the family solicitors' gloomy office, and pondered on its strength of jaw and impenetrable cast.

The grey eyes, thoughtfully narrowed at this moment, were pale and glittery against the deep tan of lean, grooved cheeks. They exactly matched the paleness of the man's tropic-weight grey suit, Maddie noted, subconsciously approving its perfect cut and the way it fitted those awesomely broad shoulders. As he flicked ash impatiently into a large, mulga-wood ashtray on Mr. James Opal's desk, she noticed that his fingers were long and brown, the nails well cared for. He was a long, brown, impatient sort of man altogether, she decided judicially, wishing now that the cold grey eyes weren't fastened upon her in quite such an unfriendly fashion.

Beneath the window, with its nondescript cream lace frill that did no more than blur the skyscraper opposite, the traffic rumbled and roared along George Street outside. The Sydney rush was at its morning peak right now, and Maddie, who had had to hurry to this early appointment, clenched her teeth on an impending yawn, and hoped she gave an impression of businesslike alertness and vigour, both of which qualities positively exuded from the occupant of the other chair. They came at her in overwhelming waves, those qualities, as the grey eyes clashed with hers again in a way that made Maddie quite breathless, and caused a steely cymbal of warning to clang the last sleepy cobwebs from her brain.

Mr. James Opal, of Opal, Rose and Heming, adjusted his spectacles, and plunged tactfully into the breach, as if aware that the build-up of tension had become almost explosive.

He cleared his throat, picked up the typewritten sheets in front of him.

'Shall I – er – just refresh you both on the – er – salient points, then, Miss Masterton?' he queried, and without waiting for her further assent, proceeded to do so in a flat, legal voice.

'—being of sound mind, do hereby bequeath to my only daughter Madeleine Janet Masterton the property of Yatta-billa and the residue of my estate, apart from the aforemen-tioned individual bequests, providing that the said Madeleine Janet Masterton, at present believed to be domi-ciled in England, fulfils a term of one year's residence on Yattabilla, as earnest of her intention to inherit, and to cher-ish the property in the manner in which I myself have en-deavoured to do, without the physical assistance or moral support or either herself or her mother during this past number of years. In the event that, either, my executors are unable to contact my daughter within six months of my decease, or, having been contacted, my daughter for any reason defaults in thereafter fulfilling a period of one year's continuous residence on Yattabilla, I bequeath the property in its entirety to my neighbour Stephen Gainsborough Darley in appreciation of his invaluable friendship and con-cern during my illness.'

Mr. Opal stopped speaking, and surveyed his listeners.

'Well, Miss Masterton? Mr. Darley?'

Maddie opened her mouth, closed it again. She felt a curious tide of unreality swamping over and about her.

'Something to your advantage,' they had said when they contacted her in London, adding that her passage would be paid from her late father's estate.

'Something to your advantage.'

Maddie could still remember the morning that that phrase dropped into her life as vividly as if it were yester-day, instead of two whole months, several oceans, a whole hemisphere, away. After all, it had been bound to make an impact, hadn't it? Especially when you happened to be a struggling stenographer, with minimum shorthand speeds and a little brother to care for as well.

Maddie hadn't mentioned the little brother yet — not to anyone.

Even Mr. James Opal, of Opal, Rose and Heming, did not know about Skeet, and neither did Mr. Stephen Gainsborough Darley.

It almost seemed as if her very own father hadn't known about Skeet, either, and that was something that puzzled Maddie very much right now. It not only puzzled her. It added to her sense of unreality, because Skeet was so alive, so full of mischief and fun, so demanding, so *expensive*, that to Maddie he was the only reality in this whole impossible situation. It was her father, Mr. Opal, Stephen Darley, Yattabilla itself, that were the dream!

Skeet had been Maddie's reason for making the long sea trip from the familiar comfort of the dingy London scene to this sprawling, turbulent, heat-hazed city, with its ink-blue harbour and gracefully arched bridge; its still-new skyscrapers and teeming inhabitants, the girls gaily clad, with a slim, brown-legged gaudiness against the blazing gold of the Australian sun, the men bronzed and casual after the formality to which she was accustomed. Lots of them wore shorts, even in the city. Here everything was new compared with the drab ancience of the British capital. The buildings, the jetties, the pavements, the gardens, the statues, all had a quality of newness that belied a mere hundred and seventy years or so. There was an all-pervading feeling of excitement, adventure, experiment, in the air, as of a great city emerging from urban adolescence into cosmopolitan adulthood.

Maddie had sensed that excitement immediately, and was aware of its momentous nature. She felt caught up in it already, as though her own life was somehow bound up in its pulsing promise of great things to come. She wished she could communicate her new awareness to Skeet, too, but of course he was too young to understand.

7

He just looked about him, at the bridge and the sea and the ferry-boats and the yachts, with wonder in his wistful blue eyes, and trust on his pale, freckled face. Trust for *her*, for Maddie. Trust that she had done the right thing for them both in bringing him across the world to this frighteningly strange, hot city.

Now Maddie was wondering if Skeet's trust had been misplaced.

Had she done the right thing, after all? She had never envisaged that 'something to your advantage' might not be a cash legacy at all, but a derelict station away in the never-never, where she and Skeet would have to endure a year of what sounded incredibly like a prison sentence.

And after that year – what?

It had taken all of her savings to pay for Skeet's passage, beyond a little that she had retained as what she called 'safety money'.

She wondered, now, about Yattabilla – about all the implications.

There seemed little doubt that the property itself *was* derelict – or the house, at any rate – because Stephen Darley had ground out his cigarette-end, and was saying tersely, finally,

'It's preposterous! I've said that all along! Miss Masterton could never live there! It's absolutely out of the question, even for a year.'

His voice, in the last sentence, had reverted to its deep, pleasant, drawling sound, but even when it drawled, it had an edge to it. The edge matched up with the coolness in the narrowed grey eyes.

'*Why* is it preposterous?' asked Maddie, suddenly, perversely in disagreement, although a moment ago she had been inwardly shuddering at the mere idea.

Something about this man disturbed her, and put her on the defensive. Perhaps it was his decisiveness, his self-assurance, as though he was accustomed to having his orders obeyed and his utterances unchallenged.

8

Maddie was challenging them now, and he did not appear to like that.

An impatient frown gathered on his teak-brown forehead, bringing his thick black brows together in a disapproving scowl.

'Because, Miss Masterton, your father never did a thing to that homestead, that's why. Not one solitary repair did he do after your mother ran out on him.'

'She did *not* run out on him!' Maddie was indignant.

Stephen Darley leaned back in his chair and raised one brow, very expressively – *horribly* expressively, it seemed to Maddie – then he fished in his pocket for the makings, and began to roll himself another cigarette.

'We won't argue about that, if you don't mind,' he retorted imperturbably, as one might brush aside the remark of an ignorant child.

'But I do mind! I – I won't have you sitting there, suggesting that my mother – that she—'

'Leave it, child.' That was a command – quietly and courteously spoken, but a command, nevertheless.

Maddie, effectively silenced, watched helplessly, but with a reluctant interest, as tobacco was rubbed between calm brown palms and tilted deftly on to a wafer-thin sliver of paper. Wretchedly, she noted the absence of even the tiniest tremor in the lean, tanned fingers that were fashioning the neat cylinder so capably, then bringing the finished article to the man's lips.

She herself was shivering with reaction – a combination of shock and anticlimax and the knowledge that she had let Skeet down after all.

'You're overwrought,' Stephen Darley observed, when he had drawn on his cigarette to his satisfaction. 'Furthermore, I suspect you have only the haziest knowledge of the subject in question – and indeed, it's quite irrelevant to the present discussion. The fact remains, that, for *whatever* reasons, Yattabilla homestead is in an unthinkable state for a sheltered young English girl, unused to either the conditions or the climate.'

Maddie's oval chin tilted ominously.

'I'm not English,' she corrected coldly. 'I was *born* on Yattabilla, so that makes me as Australian as you are yourself.'

'Can you remember anything about it?' He shot the question at her abruptly.

'N-no, not really. But I – I remember my mother telling me that I was born out in the country.'

'The country! You make it sound like an afternoon jaunt down to Sussex!' He shifted his weight impatiently in the small leather chair. 'You can't remember, Miss Masterton, because you happened to be a mere child when your mother ran out on Gerald Masterton, and from what I can gather, she took you straight to England, which makes you English by habit and upbringing, and totally unsuited to roughing it out in the *country* here.'

Maddie hated the way he stressed that word. She hated his whole, disparaging attitude.

He was obviously trying to rattle her, to shake her already dwindling confidence. He didn't want her to come to Yattabilla, that much was certain. Of course, he *wouldn't*, though, would he, in the circumstances? If she did not come, if she could somehow frighten her off, the property would come to him in due course. Maddie glanced at his set, stern features, wishing that she could read the unreadable. If she could, she was pretty sure that her guess would be right, and that was why he was being so obstructive just now.

'The property itself, the – er – station? Is it in good order, or is it, too, in a *derelict* condition?' Maddie couldn't keep the sarcasm from her voice.

Stephen Darley regarded her gravely. His eyes did not waver.

'No. The property itself is anything but derelict – quite the reverse, in fact. Your father's loneliness drove him on and on, but his energies were all directed to affairs outside the homestead, Miss Masterton. I expect his memories *inside* it were too painful to dwell upon, but anyway, his efforts to improve the place paid off. Yattabilla is a station in extremely good going order. Your father laid on plenty of bores, and they are in excellent condition. Water means everything once you get out into those parts, and your father secured his position in that respect to the best of his ability. Yattabilla is well watered, and well stocked, and Yattabilla steers have a well-deserved name at the sale yards. After a spell on a fattening property, they do well at the abattoirs, too. As regards the sheep stock, it's in a strong-wool area, with an unavoidable dust and burr problem, but your father was improving that aspect steadily, and his wool-clip was by no means to be sneezed at, and increasing every year.'

'I see.' Maddie hadn't the faintest idea about steers and abattoirs and burrs and wool-clips, but not for the world would she have shown her ignorance to the hatefully well-informed Stephen Darley!

A faint smile relieved the sternness of his weathered features.

'I doubt if you do, actually,' he retorted mildly, but with a disconcertingly cynical accuracy.

Maddie flushed.

'I see that it could be a *desirable* property, anyway,' she returned pointedly, stung by his perception. She wanted to hurt him just then, wanted to wipe away that confidence, erase that – that – smugness!

His firm lips tightened.

'It *is* a desirable property, Miss Masterton,' he agreed coolly, 'especially, as you are no doubt thinking, to the owner of the neighbouring station. Together they could be quite an outfit, couldn't they, and moreover very convenient to run as a single holding? I realize that that's what you're hinting. That, however, has little bearing on your own particular problem, does it – the derelict homestead?'

The grey eyes were crinkling a little bit at the corners, almost as if they were thinking of smiling. If they smiled now, it would be a triumphant smile, Maddie knew that for sure.

Oh, Skeet, Skeet, what have I landed us in? she was thinking desperately. Where, now, was the pulsing promise, the glowing sense of adventure?

'I have no problem, Mr. Darley,' she informed him coldly, rashly, 'although I do appreciate your apparent concern.' She turned back to the waiting Mr. Opal. 'I intend to fulfil the conditions of my father's will, and claim my inheritance,' she continued proudly. 'Perhaps you will be good enough to furnish me with all the necessary details, if I call back at a convenient time?'

'Of course, of course, Miss Masterton. The decision rests with you alone, although you may find it – er – advisable, even necessary, to alter your mind during the course of the – er – the period of residence. Most unwise. Most unwise. I shall do nothing to dissuade you, but I cannot help feeling—' here a reproving shake of the head '—that you would do well to heed Mr. Darley's views. He was, after all, one of your father's closest acquaintances, and is a trustee of the estate in addition.'

Stephen Darley had risen from his chair.

Standing, his height and breadth were formidable. The office suddenly seemed smaller, suffocating, claustrophobic.

'I – I shall return tomorrow to discuss the journey,' Maddie said rather breathlessly, and with a formal nod, managed a fairly dignified exit that cloaked a curious weakness in her limbs.

As she clattered down the dark stairs, and out into the glare of the street, her mind was beating a tattoo in her brain.

What have I done? What have I done?

Oh, Skeet! It's too late to turn back now!

Maddie plunged into the crowd, felt a firm hand taking her arm, and looked up to find the Darley man at her side.

'I want to talk to you,' he said as he piloted her across the busy street. 'Perhaps you would care for a cup of coffee?'

'No, thank you,' she returned formally, grateful that she had a genuine excuse. 'I have to meet someone. I've already been much longer than I'd thought.'

Skeet would be waiting for her at the milk bar where she had left him.

'May I call on you, then, at your apartment? Where are you staying?'

'It's a good way out from the city centre, I'm afraid,' she hedged. 'And there's nothing, really, that we have to say to each other in any case – not for a year, anyway!' added Maddie wickedly, because she resented his domineering manner and still longed to assert herself.

The hand on her arm tightened viciously. The lean fingers bit into her flesh so savagely and suddenly that she almost winced aloud. She knew that she had struck home with that last remark.

She was halted then and there, and pulled round abruptly, face to face with Stephen Darley, while the people jostled past. His expression was carefully inscrutable. Only those biting fingers had revealed his annoyance.

'You will meet me for dinner tonight, Miss Masterton. I have only a couple more days left. We'll go somewhere quiet, but as your father's friend and trustee, there are certain points to be cleared up, and that's just what I mean to do, so don't put me off with more excuses. We know virtually nothing about you, remember. At what time, and where, shall I call for you?'

Maddie looked up and met an imperious grey gaze. It was quite useless to argue, she could see that!

'You don't need to call for me,' she replied evasively, thinking of the dingy boarding-house – of Skeet, too. 'I shall be waiting for you wherever you say.'

'The Blue Balcony, then, at eight.'

Before she had time to more than nod, he had left her.

Maddie could see his tall, tanned, grey-clad figure, making its way through the crowd towards the next pedestrian crossing. Only the bruise which was beginning to throb on her soft upper arm reminded her of her promised dinner date later. The Blue Balcony, at eight. Maddie had a feeling that she was not going to enjoy her evening out!

When she reached the milk bar, Skeet was sitting at one of the little tables, disconsolately fingering the bent straw in his empty glass. His freckled face brightened at her approach.

'You were an awfully long time, Maddie. I spent my last ten cents ages ago. Can I have another milk-shake? A pineapple one this time?'

She ordered one, and an ice-cream soda for herself, and carried the two drinks back to the table.

'Did it go all right, Maddie? Is everything going to be all right?' The child's pale face was taut and anxious. Although, at ten years of age, he couldn't possibly understand all the implications, he had sensed his sister's own tension, had realized that they were both on the brink of some new decision, and that Maddie had been strangely apprehensive and worked up when she had left him earlier this morning.

'Yes, darling, it's going to be all right,' Maddie told him reassuringly.

Then she smiled at him, and Skeet felt better, because Maddie had a very lovely smile indeed. It curled her wide, sensitive mouth at the corners, and showed two rows of pretty, even, white teeth. It made tawny lights dance in her sherry-coloured eyes, too, and brought a tinge of colour to the flawless, creamy skin of her cheeks and throat. Sitting there in her simple green shift, with her blonde hair hanging straight and silky to her shoulders, even Skeet could see that she was very pretty, really. He betted everyone else thought so, too. He had seen people looking at her when she came in just now, the way they always did. You had to admit that her hair was eye-catching, with that lovely natural honey colour.

He smiled back at his sister, and pulled again at the straw, drawing in his cheeks as he did so, watching with satisfaction as the yellow liquid ran up the straw, and then back again, as he blew instead of sucking. There was a noisy gurgle and a pleasing froth, but Maddie frowned at him, and her smile went away.

She seemed kind of preoccupied, because she didn't openly rebuke him – just sat there staring at her own soda drink without speaking.

'Did you see the man?' prodded Skeet curiously.

'Mm? Yes. Yes, I saw him. I saw two of them, in fact. I have to see one of them again tonight, Skeet. You'll be all right with Mrs. Prowse till I get back, won't you? You could watch her television if you asked her nicely, I'm sure.'

'Yes, I could, couldn't I!' Skeet was obviously pleased at the prospect. 'Mrs. Prowse is nice, I think. But I don't like Barney. I hope he's not there.'

Barney was their landlady's son, a gangling youth of thirteen, who enjoyed annoying Skeet by calling him 'pommy' all the time.

'He'll probably be doing his homework,' comforted Maddie. 'Anyway, Skeet, you'll have to be a bit tougher, and learn not to mind what people say. You won't have to put up with him much longer, because we're going away soon. We're going away on a great big adventure.'

'Gee, Maddie! D'you mean – leaving Sydney? We've only just got here!'

'Yes, I know, but we're going to return to the place where I was born, Skeet. Remember, I told you? It's called Yattabilla. We're going to have a home of our very own, not lodgings in a stuffy old boarding-house with no garden and no view.'

'Gee!' Skeet was impressed. He sucked the last of the pineapple mixture up the straw noisily and then asked offhandedly, 'What will Robert say, Maddie? Will he be coming too?'

Maddie felt her colour rising. She, too, had been thinking about Robert Manners. It was going to be difficult, leaving

Robert, because she had come to depend on him for moral support in her moments of uncertainty.

They had met on the ship coming out to Australia. Robert had joined from Durban, and had immediately drawn close to the two lost-looking young people on his own deck. He had just completed a surveying mission for a project in Cape Province, and was ready to relax and allow himself to be caught up in the revelries and superficial acquaintanceships that typify a brief sea-voyage.

He was a clean-limbed, fair young man of twenty-six, and this had been his first trip abroad. It had been a successful mission in every way, and there was already a hint of possible promotion for him when he reported back to his firm in Sydney. He hadn't intended any deep involvement when he struck up a friendship with Maddie and Skeet, but he soon found that her wistful air of uncertainty was oddly appealing. It aroused feelings in Robert that he hadn't known he possessed – manly, protective feelings that made him want to shelter Maddie, because he had a horrid suspicion, from what she had told him, that she was on a wild goose chase, and would have been far better advised to remain in London, bashing a typewriter with her firm of importers.

It wasn't very long before Robert realized that he had fallen in love with this slender, fine-boned girl, with the sherry eyes that danced in those fleeting moments when her expression of anxiety gave way to gaiety, and that curtain of silk-fine hair that was the envy of every other woman on board. The nicest thing about Maddie – the thing that had really won Robert – was her complete ignorance of her own charms or the effect they had on him. Several times he had been on the verge of confessing to his emotional state, and on each occasion he had stifled the impulse. Keep it light for now, he told himself, with the native caution that was a part of his character. Perhaps, when he got back to Sydney, heard just how far his promotion might take him, got his hoped-for increase in salary, he could think more seriously about offering Maddie something more lasting and worthwhile than the present set-up. In the meantime, it was better to maintain a rather more brotherly angle. Not for anything would he have caused that anxious, wistful air of Maddie's to deepen into even greater apprehension!

Robert had been a hundred per cent successful in cloaking his feelings. Thinking about him now, Maddie was aware only of a sinking regret that she would have to part from him before they'd really got to know each other.

Life was like that, she supposed. Just when you met someone rather special, who seemed to be on your own wavelength, you got whisked away on some new adventure, so that you never knew about the 'might-have-been'.

It was debatable, too, if a year at Yattabilla could be termed an adventure – not an agreeable one, anyway, although for Skeet's sake she must try to pretend that it was. If she didn't manage to regard it in that light, her courage might fail her altogether!

'Robert?' she said now, abstractedly, in answer to Skeet. 'No, he won't be coming, Skeet, not to Yattabilla. He's got things of his own to do right here in Sydney. Remember, he's been away for quite a long time, too. He'll have a lot to catch up on.'

'Oh.' Skeet sounded depressed. 'Will it be just you and me, then, Maddie?'

'Yes, Skeet, just you and me. It will be fun! An adventure!'

Maddie tried to sound bright and convincing, even though little butterflies of dread were fluttering around inside her.

'Does he know we're going?'

'Robert? I'll have to tell him. I'm going to see him tomorrow night, so I shall tell him then.'

'Will you be out *two* nights in a row, Maddie?'

'I'm afraid so, darling. I didn't know about tonight, you see, when I said I'd meet Robert. But after that we'll be together all the time, at Yattabilla. You can watch Mrs. Prowse's television, Skeet. I know she'll let you.'

Her brother followed her dolefully from the milk bar.

'I hope Barney has lots of homework – *both* nights,' he evinced miserably.

Maddie ignored that. There were times when she just had to ignore the things Skeet said, because she was helpless to do anything about them.

This was one of those times. She *had* to meet that rather frightening Mr. Darley tonight. He had been insistent, and there was no point in avoiding the issue. In a way, he did have a certain moral claim to information, she supposed, since he appeared to have known her father better than anyone else, and was an appointed trustee, moreover. And she *had* to see Robert before she left Sydney. One couldn't just disappear without saying goodbye to someone who had been as good to her as he had. It might be difficult to make him understand, though. He had thought her quest from London to Sydney to be too frivolously uncertain to warrant giving up the small measure of security she had won for herself and Skeet, so what he would think when she told him about Yattabilla was all too predictable!

Once they were on the bus, Skeet cheered up. They went right to the top, near the front, where he could look down on the beetling, bright roofs of the cars streaking along beneath them, and ahead right up the crawling length of William Street to the Cross at the end of the straight. There they hopped off, and went into one of the numerous delicatessens, where Maddie bought some sandwiches and cold sliced sausage. She had tomatoes and some cucumber in their room at the boarding-house, and Mrs. Prowse had given her the use of an electric kettle for tea-making, since she didn't 'do' meals, she explained, except breakfast which was all in with the lodging bill.

Maddie had discovered that eating meals out could be a very expensive business, which was why she now made herself and Skeet as cheerful a picnic as she could in their room. Then she took him walking down to Rushcutter's Bay.

The little boy would have liked to stay there longer.

There were yachts bobbing out on the sparkly green water, and people playing tennis, and swings to swing on in the play-park. Maddie had to use all her powers of persuasion to urge him back with her to the rented room, so that she could wash her hair and prepare for her evening appointment.

She dressed with meticulous care that evening. She wasn't quite sure why, except that it was necessary to impress Mr. Stephen Darley, somehow, and to bolster her own shaky confidence.

She opened the cheap, veneered wardrobe, and regarded her few dresses hesitating.

The Blue Balcony. Maddie had passed it, although she hadn't of course been inside. It ran the full length of the second floor of a building overlooking some beautiful gardens, with the harbour in the background, and its long French windows opened on to a wide wrought-iron balcony, where people could be seen sitting under a milky glitter of stars in the warm night air. The entire façade of the balcony was picked out in blue and gilt, and the windows were framed by heavy chintz curtains with gold fringed edges. From within floated the muted sounds of music, and from time to time one caught a glimpse of white-jacketed waiters hovering attentively over the tables inside, or balancing trays of drinks for those on the terrace.

Maddie lifted her best dress from its hanger. It was a simply swathed, brief-skirted affair of navy chiffon, with long transparent sleeves, and it had cost Maddie a whole two weeks' salary from a shop in Regent Street. It had been her sole extravagance, and amid the cotton-clad gaiety of the tourist throng on board ship, it had seemed an unwarranted one – one of those stupidly impulsive buys about which one has later regrets.

Now, she was grateful for its morale-boosting perfection. She clipped ear-studs in her lobes – her only adornment apart from her wristwatch – and set about contriving a sophisticated hairstyle by sweeping her hair up from her nape, and securing it with the aid of a small matching switch.

That way it made her appear older, more assured, she thought with satisfaction. Maddie couldn't be expected to know that the nape of her neck, now gracefully exposed, looked extraordinarily young and vulnerable. Her quick glance in the mirror did not reveal that fact. It only reflected her creamy skin against the dark, complimenting navy, and the golden sheen of her hair beneath the pallid electric bulb.

Maddie made up her eyes with care and subtlety, touched gentle colour to her lips, and went to say goodnight to Skeet.

'You'll promise to go to bed at half-past nine, Skeet?'

'Ten, Maddie? Couldn't it be ten? After all, *you're* going out and having fun, aren't you?' He eyed her reproachfully, hopefully.

'Ten, then, Skeet,' agreed Maddie weakly. She sometimes thought she was too lenient with Skeet. It had something to do with trying to make up for his having no parents.

Fun! If only he knew!

Closing the door quietly behind her, Maddie went to catch a bus back into the city.

CHAPTER TWO

IT was a rebuff to discover that Stephen Darley had not even bothered to change into something more formal than the pale grey tropic-weight suit of the morning. Even so, she was aware, as she followed the waiter over a sea of soft carpet to a small table in an alcove, that her escort possessed an air of distinction and ease of bearing that drew the eyes of other diners to him as he saw her seated, and then took possession of the plush, padded leather bench opposite her.

If he was at all aware of a social lapse in not being as formally attired as others about him, he gave no sign, and there was certainly nothing apologetic about the imperious way in which he signalled to the head waiter, who came hurrying over, volubly attentive.

'Good evening, Meestair Darley. And what is your wish tonight?'

Stephen Darley ran a practised eye down a long menu whose list of tempting dishes appeared to Maddie endless, and in a gourmet class to which she was totally unaccustomed.

'Oysters, Luigi?'

'Yes indeed, Meestair Darley. The best. The sweetest.'

'You care for them, Miss Masterton?'

Maddie blushed faintly.

'I've never tasted them,' she felt bound to admit.

'No?' His eyes travelled over the elegant, upswept hair, the sophisticated swathe of navy chiffon, and came to rest at that girlishly vulnerable throat in a way that made Maddie feel overdressed and foolish. He turned back to the waiter then, saying easily,

'In that case, we'll have them cooked, Luigi. Oysters Kilpatrick, the consommé, and chicken Leonora.'

Maddie was relieved that the decision had been made for her, even while she struggled with annoyance, too. She would have liked to look longer at that amazing menu. It would have been something to tell Skeet, only Stephen Darley was so obviously accustomed to taking command that he had whisked it away. Apparently he saw no reason to consult others over their personal preferences.

Grudgingly, she had to admit that his choice was perfect.

The oysters were succulent, delicious in their crispy cloak of bacon. The soup was steaming hot and appetizing, the chicken pure delight.

There was a pleasant interval between each course, and Maddie sipped cautiously at her tall-stemmed glass of dry white wine, and watched the couples who came and went, passing their table on their way to the small area of dancing space. Mr. Darley, of course, did not ask her to dance – she hadn't expected him to. As she watched him eating his meal, she was conscious that an air of remote politeness existed between them. It was only slightly more comfortable than that edge of concealed antagonism.

He ate as if he were genuinely hungry, without self-consciousness. When he looked up and caught her watching him, he must have read her thoughts.

His grin was sudden, boyish, and for the first time there was a hint of an apology in his tone.

'I'm sorry to be making such a glutton of myself. I've been in a hurry all day – a series of appointments. I hadn't time for much in the way of food.'

Maddie met his eyes and saw the grey glint of humour there, a call for a temporary truce. She saw, too, for the first time, that there were tired shadows about them, and that the little lines that fanned out from the corners were more deeply etched than she had supposed them in the morning. His mouth, when unrelaxed, was taut with fatigue.

He must be a very important man, to have appointments right through the day and responsibilities that didn't allow him time off even to eat, and one of those responsibilities had been to do with the entrustment of her own father's estate – one of the appointments, too!

Maddie felt a brief wave of compunction and uncontrolled sympathy. She felt she had been allowed a tiny glimpse behind the man's barrier of reserve and inscrutability, and what she had sensed there had been *almost* human.

Maddie, in fact, was so pleased that she had had that tiny peep into the nature of the man, even fleetingly, that she smiled. It was the wide, complete, beautiful curling smile that Skeet secretly admired. She had no idea, of course, that it warmed her little brother through and through like a spreading rush of golden sun. She didn't know that her sherry-brown eyes softened and laughed, too, with the curling of her expressively mobile mouth, or that her teeth glinted pearly-white against the pale coral colour of her lips.

Just for a split second, Stephen Darley's hand was arrested in its function of conveying food neatly to his mouth. It was a moment of utter stillness, when even the carved granite planes of his face, the severe outline of his head and shoulders, were as still and quiet and thoughtful as the Sphinx itself.

Or maybe Maddie had imagined that pause?

'Don't apologize, Mr. Darley. I do understand – and one would have to be blasé indeed not to enjoy such a delicious meal!'

He inclined his head politely. The reserve was back.

'You'd better call me Steve,' he told her, then, formally, 'since we will of necessity be seeing a certain amount of each other in the future – and I shall call you Madeleine. No need to ask *your* name. We had the devil of a search for Madeleine Janet Masterton, I can assure you – it's a name I'm not likely to forget in a hurry!'

No truce after all! thought Maddie. He resented her. He would always be annoyed with her for turning up at all!

'And are you still intending to pursue this madness?' he asked abruptly, when Luigi had set their pineapple before them with a flourish.

'I don't see that it's madness,' she argued stubbornly, her eyes on her plate, hardly noticing or appreciating the delicious tang of the cold fresh fruit against her palate. 'That is, unless you're suggesting that my father was mad in making this stipulation?'

He looked at her, then, very gravely indeed.

'I'm not implying any such thing, Madeleine. Gerald – your father – was my friend. A valued friend.' He hesitated, searching for words, still holding her eyes with his. 'The thing *you*'ve got to remember is that he was also a very lonely man, particularly towards the end, when he was too ill to go on employing sheer physical effort and pre-occupation as a means of escape from his personal loneliness. His domestic life was inevitably an unbalanced one, and possibly his judgement became a trifle unbalanced, too. Otherwise—' he offered her a tailor-made cigarette from a slim silver case, took one himself when she declined '—otherwise he would have been more awake to the complete unsuitability of his suggestion. He had little idea of the type of girl his only daughter might turn out to be. It was quite unrealistic to expect a young thing, city-reared at that, to take on the occupancy of a crumbling station-homestead, even for a year.'

He cupped his hand to his lighter, pulled on his cigarette, and exhaled. With his head thrown back, he gave her a level, extraordinarily persuasive glance.

'Will you see reason, or do I have to make you?'

'Black coffee, madam?' That was Luigi. If he hadn't interrupted at that particular moment, Maddie might have been really rude.

When Luigi had departed, she replied with deceptive mildness,

'You can't make me, can you, Mr. – er – Steve? I think you may have very good reasons for *not* wanting me to come

24

to Yattabilla, but the final choice is mine, isn't it? That's what Mr. Opal told me, at any rate, and my intention remains firm. I hope you didn't invite me out for dinner tonight for the sole purpose of altering my mind, because if so, I'm afraid you've been unsuccessful.'

Steve did not answer immediately. Instead he smoked in thoughtful silence.

Maddie found his poise unnerving. He was a difficult adversary to cope with, no matter how hard one tried, and she was rather hopelessly aware that he knew far more about what she intended taking on than she did herself. It was both annoying and humiliating not to be able to ask all the questions she was curious to have answered for her. What was the Yattabilla place *really* like, for instance? Where was it? How remote?

Lilting music wafted around them as Maddie sat primly, all her questions unasked.

Watching with a secret pang of envy the diners about her, she noted that they were couples or foursomes who were obviously enjoying each other's company far more than she and her own companion. Some young things were dancing close, with every appearance of being deeply in love. Others were more circumspect, probably on the brink of a more tender attachment, the way she and Robert might have been – but for that year at Yattabilla, which was soon to take her away.

She leaned back against the soft upholstery behind her, letting the music wash over her and ease away some of her tension.

Steve Darley appeared to be still preoccupied. Maddie studied the stern angles of his profile covertly, looked at the hand lying carelessly along the table where he had half-turned in his seat to stretch out his legs more comfortably. It was a squarish hand, broad over the back, with long, square-tipped fingers that for all their strength had a certain sensitivity. Remembering that biting grip of his this morning, she wondered idly what it would be like to be held in those arms – properly held, like those young lovers over there, for instance. Would he be capable of tenderness, sympathy? Maddie doubted it. His love would have to be one of mastery and subjection.

'A liqueur, Madeleine?' Steve's voice broke into her thoughts.

Luigi was back again, hovering.

'P – pardon?'

'Cointreau for the lady, and my usual brandy, Luigi, please.'

'I – didn't really want one;' she murmured a trifle ungraciously, as Luigi darted off. He might have at least waited for her to *say*, she thought resentfully.

'Nonsense. It will do you good,' he contradicted brusquely, surveying her with narrowed eyes. 'The wine helped a little, but you're not at ease with me, are you, Madeleine?'

Maddie felt embarrassed colour assail her cheeks.

'You aren't a very easy person,' she mumbled incoherently. 'You d-don't *make* things very easy.'

'I could,' he retorted more gently, 'if you would allow me. But you won't, will you? You've put a mental barricade up between us, and that cancels out whatever I say – isn't that so? In fact, you're scared stiff of me! You've been as terrified as a rabbit since the moment we came in, and I'm wondering why?' He smiled faintly. 'The female sex don't find me quite so overwhelmingly unapproachable as a rule!'

Maddie's cheeks were on fire. The wine had given her a heady glow, a feeling of unfamiliar recklessness.

'I – think you're being beastly!' she flashed, with a show of spirit. 'You've been amusing yourself at my expense the whole evening, haven't you? And as for the reputation with the female sex upon which you no doubt pride yourself, as far as I'm concerned, I'm perfectly satisfied that you remain unapproachable, if you want my candid opinion!'

'Touché!' A reluctant grin spread over his tanned features. His teeth were white, and their crookedness was oddly attractive, she had to admit, even if his self-conceit was deplorable.

Steve lit another cigarette, sipped his brandy. Then—

'Let's forget the personal angle just now, then, shall we?' he drawled with deceptive pleasantness. 'That, I'm afraid, brings us right back to where we came in! Madeleine, I'm going to make a suggestion that I want you to consider seriously, and that is that you pass up this whole crazy scheme. Contest your father's will, if you like. As his daughter, you have certain legal rights. You could be successful if you go about things in the right way.'

Maddie saw that he was utterly sincere – or that he *seemed* so, at any rate. Leaning towards her to stress his point, eyes fixed gravely upon her face, it was difficult to believe that he was being anything but genuine.

'Do you think, then, that my father was – that he *wasn't* of sound mind when he made that will?' she asked. 'Could I contest it on the grounds of – well, insanity?'

It was hard to bring out that word in connection with her very own father, even though she couldn't even remember him. She felt vaguely disloyal, unfair to the shadowy picture of an ill, frustrated, disappointed and lonely man.

'No, I don't think that at all. I've told you already. He was simply misguided. It was an error of judgement, clearly.'

She was silent, considering.

Error of judgement or not, she couldn't do things Steve's way. It cost money to take legal proceedings, and it might be months and months before anything was settled. There was also the very real possibility that she might lose the action, too, and she would already have forfeited the chance of a year's residence. She'd have lost everything! Mr. Opal had said that she must be at Yattabilla within six months of her father's death, as 'earnest of her intention to inherit'. Yes, those had been his words, and four of those months had gone already. It had taken the Sydney people nearly two to track

27

her down in London, and then a further eight weeks to get ready for the journey and come out on the boat.

No, it was impossible. She couldn't do things Steve's way, because she couldn't run the risk of possible failure. For herself, yes, but not for Skeet. How could she possibly support Skeet and at the same time fight a legal action? And why was Stephen Darley so keen for her to do things this way? How did she know that, whatever he said right now, he might not seek to have the will upheld? He had everything to gain by doing just that. He would be a formidable opponent; a wealthy one, too. Maddie shuddered at the mere idea.

'Come on, Madeleine, you can see it's sense. You can't possibly go out and live alone on Yattabilla. You haven't the foggiest notion of what's involved, have you? Just admit it, and we'll get down to the alternatives, there's a good girl.'

Steve's voice was cajoling, almost kind.

Maddie swallowed. She *wished* she could trust him, but she knew she couldn't. He was a hard-boiled businessman, wasn't he – the sort who had appointments all day when he came to the city, important appointments that allowed him no time even to eat! He wasn't the kind to hand over a property like Yattabilla on a plate! The house might be derelict (she found herself even doubting him on *that* score, too), but hadn't he admitted that the cattle were a satisfactory source of income, and the wool-clip increasing? He must have some ulterior motive in urging her to take this latest, unorthodox step. Maybe he even *knew* that she would lose her case, and that it would be the quickest way to dispose of her and claim the place for himself.

Doubts assailed Maddie afresh. She found herself meeting those concerned, level grey eyes and simply *longing* to trust him, but she fought against the feeling, although she would certainly have welcomed a shoulder to lean on just then! She had never felt more alone – except for Skeet, of course.

Maddie braced herself. She had been subconsciously

nerving herself, all evening, to tell Stephen Darley about Skeet, and this seemed like as good a time as any to do it.

'I won't be *alone* on Yattabilla, actually,' she stated, trying now to sound very casual.

'No?' The black brows opposite rose sceptically. 'Who'll be with you, Madeleine? Don't tell me the lady has a husband stowed away somewhere? With that untouched look about you, I simply won't believe it!'

'There's Skeet.' She couldn't even joke, her voice felt too stifled.

'Skeet?' He had stopped smiling.

'Yes – Skeet,' croaked Maddie. She was making a bad job of this!

'And who exactly is Skeet?' Steve was asking carefully. Funny how such a big, athletic man could sit so very still. His words dropped like pebbles into the stillness that he himself had created.

'Skeet's my brother.'

'Your – *brother*!' His exclamation was startled, incredulous. It was evident that, whatever he had been expecting her to say, it certainly had not been that. 'Impossible!'

'Don't *say* that,' pleaded Maddie, agonized.

Her face was dead white, her eyes huge, naked with misery and doubt. The doubt had been there ever since this morning, ever since the moment when Stephen Darley had said, 'You were a mere child when your mother ran out on Gerald Masterton.' It had haunted her right through the day, through the picnic in the room, and the walk to the Bay, and swinging on the swings, and everything. It had been with her all the time she was getting ready for this rendezvous, and it had caused her to give Skeet a clinging sort of despairing hug when she had left him. Skeet hated being hugged, she knew that, but the dreadful doubt had made her do it.

'I'm sorry, Madeleine. I shouldn't have said that.' Steve's deep voice was contrite. 'You surprised me, that's all. I had no idea that your mother had ever married again.'

'She – didn't,' Maddie stated baldly. She knew he was looking at her, but she couldn't bring herself to meet his eyes. Instead, she let her fingers play with the tiny, fragile liqueur-glass, because she had to be doing something. 'She was a good mother, Steve,' she added in a strangled, defiant tone. 'She was *good* to Skeet and me.'

'I'm sure she was,' came the soothing, tactful murmur.

Then silence.

'She wasn't like you're thinking, Steve. She was kind and pretty and – oh, lots of fun! Maybe we didn't have much security – we never stayed in one place for very long – but we did have fun. She was always impetuous, I suppose, but gay and generous too, and we always did everything together. It was as though she was trying to make up to us for the things we didn't have – you know, a proper home, a father, and so forth.'

'What about – er – Skeet's father? Didn't he accompany you, even for a while?' he asked quietly.

Her eyes were wounded. The doubt had curled itself up into a ball at the base of her throat. She shook her head.

'There was no one – nobody like *that*, I mean. Just Mum and Skeet and me. Skeet was terribly bereft when – when we lost her. That's why I'm taking him to Yattabilla.' A pause. 'I can't remember Yattabilla, Steve – not anything about it. You said this morning that I was only a child when Mum ra— when we left, so it's understandable, I suppose.'

Silence.

'Skeet's only ten. He's a whole ten years younger than I am.' She was speaking almost to herself, as if she had forgotten the presence of the big quiet man on the other side of the table. 'If I'd been ten when we left Yattabilla, I'd remember it, wouldn't I? *Wouldn't* I?'

'Where were you when you were ten, Madeleine?'

'I can't remember. Melbourne, I think. I went to school there for a while. I was a boarder, because Mum had some sort of a job. Then we flew to England.'

'From there?'

'Yes.'

'And Skeet was born in England?'

'In London, I think. Yes, I'm sure. Mum used to say he was a true cockney – because of the Bow Bells, you know,' she added with a wan smile.

Surprisingly, Steve Darley smiled back. It was a slow, thorough, deliberate sort of smile – kind, sympathetic, very gentle. You'd almost have thought his eyes were tender. *Almost* – if you hadn't known he was a tough business type, playing poker-faced stakes for a valuable property.

'It figures, Madeleine,' he said reasonably. 'You'd be too young to know what was going on – at ten your mother would have kept it from you – but *she* returned to Yattabilla, although you didn't. She came to try for a reconciliation with Gerald, I remember that now. I was in my first year at the University at the time. She'd have left you with some friend in Melbourne, doubtless.'

'What happened?' Maddie could only whisper.

Steve shrugged.

'It didn't work out. She was there maybe a month, six weeks. Then she left – for good and all. She had to get your father's consent to take you to England, I remember. She hadn't the same problem with Skeet, it seems,' he added dryly.

'You mean—?'

'I mean that Gerald Masterton never knew he had that son, Maddie. Your mother left the country without telling him.'

'Oh-h!'

Maddie expelled her breath.

For some reason, she felt giddy, and her limbs had turned to jelly. She sat slumped against the seat, fighting back the tears which threatened. She mustn't cry in front of Stephen Darley! He was the sort who'd have very little patience with sobbing women, she was sure! She blew her nose, wiped her eyes surreptitiously, and then glared at him, wet-lashed.

'I'd have loved him just as much if he hadn't been,' she stated huskily, and surprisingly, Steve seemed to understand exactly what this oblique pronouncement meant.

'You're the loyal type, I can see,' he agreed, but there was a hint of the old irony back in his voice. 'Don't let loyalty blind your common sense, though, Madeleine. Yattabilla isn't the place for you, with, or without, Skeet. Why not pack in the idea?'

Maddie felt tired, and relieved, and emotionally confused. Maybe that's why she got so annoyed just then! Afterwards – many times afterwards – she was to wish that she had not, because it seemed to her in retrospect that that was the moment when she and Steve Darley drew wide apart, finally and irrevocably. Even the former, wary footing receded in the face of Maddie's hot words, leaving only a tenuous bridge of distrust between them.

'Don't bother to go on! Because *nothing* and *nobody* is going to stop me from going! I'd be simple if I couldn't see that it would be to your advantage if I didn't go at all, wouldn't I? It's enough that you should hint the most uncomplimentary things about my very own mother, and have me almost out of my mind all day, but you go altogether too far when you suggest that I forfeit my inheritance as well!'

After a minute of astonished silence, during which Steve Darley was obviously wrestling with his own temper, he spoke again. His words were as chill and unfriendly as the coldness in his flinty grey eyes.

'I'm sorry that that's how you feel, Madeleine. In future, I shall say nothing to imperil your youthful illusions, of that you may be sure. Even so, I doubt if you'll cherish them for very much longer!'

Stony-faced, he summoned Luigi, paid the bill, and escorted her down to the street below.

'I'll put you in a taxi,' he said coldly.

And that was just what he did! He summoned the nearest one, repeated the address she gave, squared the driver, and bowed an ironic farewell.

Maddie felt uncomfortable all the way back to the boarding-house – chastened and ashamed.

She found it difficult to get off to sleep, and when she woke up in the morning, she was unrefreshed. She took Skeet into the city again, and left him in the sunny Botanical Gardens while she saw Mr. Opal once more, and found out the best way to get to Yattabilla. It seemed that an eleven-hour train journey was involved, in order to reach the nearest township.

'I am not very certain of the exact distance of the property itself from the town of Noonday, but you will be in a better position to arrange transport for the final leg of the journey once you are actually there.' Mr. Opal regarded her with troubled eyes. 'Most of the graziers thereabouts would seem to possess their own private air-transport, Miss Masterton, and of course that simplifies the whole procedure, and cancels out the remoteness of their position to some extent. Mr. Darley, in fact, will be flying back himself shortly. If you would like me to mention that you intend making the journey yourself by a less pleasant means, I am sure he could be prevailed upon to offer you a lift?'

'Definitely not!' Maddie was horrified at the mere idea. She hoped that she would not see Stephen Darley again, ever! 'We – I'll take the train, Mr. Opal. I prefer to be independent.'

'The night train is preferable, in that case. There's an overnight sleeper service which obviates the tedium a little. I should advise you to book.'

'I'll do that,' promised Maddie.

She returned to the Gardens for Skeet, and together they made their way to the booking-office at Central Station. Her spirits sank when she learned that the sleeping berths for the next four nights were reserved already.

'I can put you on the waiting-list, Miss – Masterton, did you say the name was?'

'No, don't worry. We'll go by the day train instead.' She

was possessed of an urge to get away from Sydney now – away from the drab boarding-house, and the embarrassing memories of her evening with Steve Darley, away from Messrs. Opal, Rose and Heming, to the promise of her new life – hers and Skeet's. 'Is it possible to reserve seats – one and a child's single, Sydney to Noonday?'

'No problem, miss. The day trip is never booked up the same.'

'I'd rather be sure, though. The day after tomorrow, then, please.'

The booking-clerk wrote neatly on the reservations, punched the date on deftly, handed her the change.

When Maddie ran up the steps and into the sun once more, she found that she was clutching Skeet's hand rather tightly. She felt, now, that the step had been irrevocably taken. There was something very final about those two little cardboard tickets in her handbag – something frighteningly final.

Maddie quelled her pangs of apprehension, and took Skeet into the nearest milk-bar again. He was going to miss those milk-shakes! Or maybe he wasn't. One doubtless had milk at Yattabilla, and some fruit-flavoured syrup and an ice-cube could do the rest!

She was in a happier frame of mind when Robert called for her that evening. She felt comfortable in Robert's company. He was not so very much older than she was herself, and his views on life were youthfully uncomplicated and enthusiastic. She pushed the intrusive image of Steve Darley's cynical mouth and jaded grey eyes from her mind, and concentrated instead upon Robert's boyish charm as she was dressing for her engagement.

Tonight there was no need for special effects and impressions. This evening she could just be herself. Therefore the navy chiffon stayed where it was, and Maddie chose a full-length cotton dancing-skirt which she had made herself especially for the voyage. In the tropics its gay riot of strong colours had been appropriate, and gave a cool, fresh effect.

With it she wore a plain white shirt, and left her hair falling in its usual straight, shining curtain to her shoulders.

She had phoned Robert and broken the news of her impending departure, because she did not want their last evening to be spoiled by lectures and recriminations. After his initial disapproval had been voiced, Robert had finally agreed to say no more about it, and had invited her, instead, to come dancing with him to a nice little place he knew of.

When they arrived at the 'nice little place', she could see that it was a very grand place indeed, and it must be stretching Robert's pocket to the limit to take her there. Dear Robert! He was doing her proud on what was to be their last outing together for some time to come, and she was secretly very touched.

On the dance floor he drew her into his arms and held her tenderly.

'Sweet Maddie,' he murmured into her ear. 'I'm going to miss you, you know that?'

'Me too, Robert. But I'll write sometimes, and I hope you will too.'

'Of course. And a year will soon pass. I might even be able to come out to see you, but I don't know yet where I'll be based. They may send me off on another contract, for all I know.'

'Would you like that?'

He pulled a wry face.

'I suppose I would, except that it would prevent me seeing you as I hope to. A lot can happen in a year, though, Maddie, and by the time it's gone, my own future may be secure enough to – well, to say things to you that I can't say just now.'

Maddie's eyes had been roving casually over Robert's shoulder as they danced. Suddenly she felt herself stiffen uncontrollably in his arms.

Across the room, a head taller than most of those about him, she could see Stephen Darley. Yes, it was Steve. There was no mistaking that erect carriage and the way he held his

35

well-shaped dark head. It was tipped a little to one side just now, because he was listening to something his partner was saying, and smiling urbanely. In his dinner jacket and tucked white shirt, he looked as saturninely handsome as the Devil himself, and as far as Maddie was concerned, every bit as dangerous.

Now he was laughing with outright amusement, and the girl in his arms made a satisfied little moue. It was a co-quettish gesture, and Steve's answer was to jerk her closer, right against him, so that his face was in her hair and her head was pressed against his shoulder.

Maddie dragged her eyes away.

'Let's sit down, Robert,' she begged rather breathlessly. 'It – it's hot for dancing.'

'Aren't you feeling well, Maddie?' He was immediately concerned.

'Yes, I'm all right. It's just – maybe I'm tired.'

'It's been too much for you, this whole business. I wish you didn't have to go through with it. Surely there's some other way?'

And let that plausible villain over there get Yattabilla? Never!

'No, Rob, this is the best and only way. Truly.'

The other couple were leaving the floor now. Fortunately they were sitting on the opposite side of the long narrow room. The girl was dark, and striking rather than pretty. Her figure, in a classic floor-length gown of heavy white crepe, was as near to perfection as any Maddie had ever seen, and her skin was deeply tanned, smooth as honey. She looked like a bronze Grecian statue.

Maddie drew a sharp breath. Steve Darley was looking directly at her, across the crowded room. She knew he had seen her. There seemed to be a thread of electricity connecting them just now, and Maddie could feel its current running right through her. It wasn't a pleasant feeling. She looked away.

After that, her evening was ruined. She spent the remaining time taking pains to avoid that other couple, and it was a relief when Robert said that they must be going. At last!

To do so, they had to walk right past Steve's table, and as they did that, Maddie found her eyes drawn compulsively to him, in spite of herself. There was no answering flicker of recognition – just a bleak, blank stare – and she knew, then, that he was aware that she had purposely avoided him throughout the evening.

A couple just ahead of them blocked the way for a few moments, so that she and Robert had perforce to go on standing quite close to the others' table, waiting to pass. As they stood, the girl's voice reached her. It was smooth and resonant, with perfect pitch and diction, as one might expect of a bronze Grecian goddess!

'What unusual hair, Steve! Do look, darling! Isn't it wonful what can come out of a bottle these days? *So* foolish to meddle with nature, don't you think – and the colour's quite *fatal* with that skirt, the poor child!'

Maddie's face was aflame as she followed Robert past them to the exit. She gritted her teeth, and, wooden-faced, allowed him to hand her into a cab.

Hateful goddess! Hateful creature! They *both* were!

Maddie sank back thankfully into the comforting, concealing darkness of the taxi, glad that Robert, at least, was unaware of her humiliation.

Those cruel words, that beautiful dark head, that proud and perfect figure, would be etched on Maddie's mind for ever!

The most humbling thing of all, though, was the knowledge that Steve Darley had witnessed the whole thing. Maybe he had even been an accomplice, in thought, at least.

Maddie tried to forget the way he had been looking at the goddess before she spoke those words that had made Maddie glance away and stumble hastily forward, out of their sight. It had been a look of pride, of possession, of knowledge that his companion's flamboyant beauty was the envy of every other man in the nightclub. Steve Darley had doubtless thought it worthwhile to get out his dinner jacket for *her*, no matter how many business appointments he had had that day! And Maddie betted that *she* wouldn't be sent home, alone, in a taxi, at the end of the evening, either!

Recalling his austerely handsome face, and the way his brown hands had drawn the statuesque, white-clad girl close against him, Maddie found to her dismay that she herself was trembling.

CHAPTER THREE

SKEET licked the tips of his sticky fingers and wiped his hands on the cuffs of his khaki shorts, blatantly ignoring his sister's frown.

The carriage was full of flies and heat. It was difficult to decide which was the worse, thought Skeet morosely. Certainly the heat was there *all* the time, whereas the flies came and went.

He wondered idly where they went, in between their intermittent invasions. Maybe to the next-door compartment, where there was a baby howling, and a pungent smell of orange juice that mingled with the cloying sweetness of talcum powder whenever you walked past. Or maybe they went right outside, away from the train altogether, in search of cooler air. That's where Skeet would have gone, if he had been a fly on this train. Not that the air did look much cooler out there, but at least it would not be as boring as in here.

All day they had been trundling monotonously through the country. At first, the deep blue gorges and startling orange escarpments of the mountain ranges had provided some excitement. Skeet had felt fresh and alert, and there had been Maddie's picnic to look forward to. After the mountains, they had descended to undulating gentle slopes with shiny creeks and swaying poplars and pretty green plots of clover and lucerne.

By the time the picnic was eaten, the train was pushing its way steadily through a wheat-belt of rich red soil dotted over with bright, oily-leafed currajong trees, but that was hours and hours ago now. The picnic was finished, and so was the pretty scenery.

Both were behind them, and all that was left was a paper bag with a few bulls'-eyes in it, and a single stick of liquorice, and an endless expanse of flat, parched country, broken only by the occasional relief of an odd, small railway siding – no more than a shed, a signal-box, and sometimes a general store squatting in the shade of a few dejected eucalypts.

Skeet reached for the remaining liquorice stick, and bit a small piece. He planned to make it last, since there was nothing else but bulls'-eyes left, and he was sick of them. In fact, he was sick, full stop! The first faint queasiness had assailed his stomach a few moments ago, but Skeet resolutely ignored its warning. You had to do something, cooped up here all day, and what was there to do but read and eat? The comics were finished, so that left eating.

When the liquorice, too, was finished, he lay back and dozed. He must have actually gone to sleep, because when Maddie pulled at his shoulder to wake him up, it was completely dark. The train had slowed, and was grinding noisily over a series of points at the approach to a proper railway station.

Skeet sat up and rubbed a round peep-hole in the dust on the window-pane, peering out. You couldn't see much at all, except for a lot of lights shining out of the darkness, and a lot of people scattered along the platform, waiting for the train to come to a stop.

'Here, Skeet. Take these! Quickly!' Maddie handed him the comics, a canvas hold-all, and the bulls'-eyes. 'Put them in your pocket, and *hurry*, Skeet. We're here!'

'Here' must mean Noonday, Skeet supposed sleepily. A silly name, Noonday, especially when it was pitch dark outside. It was night in Noonday. Skeet would have giggled at that thought – would have repeated it to Maddie, but she was busy cramming the waste papers from the picnic into the small bin provided, and anyway, he was still feeling sick.

It was worse when he stood up.

Skeet pushed two of the bulls'-eyes a little desperately into his mouth, stuffed the bag into his pocket as Maddie had suggested, and followed her along the corridor. People ahead of her had already opened the door and were stepping down on to the platform.

Maddie stepped down, too, and pulled the cases after her.

'Come *on*, Skeet.'

It was quite a jump, when your legs were short with the shortness of a mere ten years.

Skeet jumped down after Maddie, and when he did so, his stomach seemed to be left hanging up there somewhere in the sky. He stood for a moment, waiting for it to subside, but it didn't. Not really. It settled somewhere in the upper part of his chest, even though he stood quite still.

'Come *on*, Skeet!'

Maddie sounded impatient. She was, in fact, hot and tired and irritable, and very uncertain, but she didn't let Skeet see that. Only her impatience showed through, because she had to get her little brother to move, to stop him just standing there holding up all the traffic.

He chewed the sweet remaining in his mouth, swallowed it, and uttered thinly,

'Maddie, I feel sick.'

'Well, you can't be sick here,' she told him with some asperity. 'We've a long way to go yet, Skeet. We've got to get out to Yattabilla somehow. Sit on that bench while I am making some inquiries, and don't – oh!' Her words faded into a gasp of pure dismay.

'Good evening, Madeleine. A comfortable journey, I trust?' Steve Darley inquired urbanely.

He had suddenly materialized out of the dispersing crowd, and stood before her, calm and debonair in a pair of pale drill trousers and an open-necked shirt with rolled-up sleeves.

Maddie, hot, sticky and dishevelled, felt at a distinct and immediate disadvantage.

'You!' she exclaimed. 'I hadn't expected to see *you*, Mr. Darley.'

'No, I can see you hadn't,' he agreed smoothly. 'And I thought we had settled for christian names. Mine's Steve, if you remember? This is all your baggage?'

He tucked a large case under one arm, took up the others and the canvas hold-all abandoned by Skeet.

'Yes, that's it. But I – I have to make some inquiries first,' she hedged breathlessly. It was humiliating not to know exactly where you were going next, or how precisely you were going to get there, especially when it happened to be the place where you'd actually been born!

Steve's face creased with amusement. As he smiled, his white teeth glinted in the yellow dimness of the platform lights.

'If you mean you want to ask where Yattabilla is, and how to get there, why not say so? And you needn't bother right now. That's why I came in to meet you. In any case, we're going no further than this tonight.'

'We?' Maddie asked coldly.

'We.' The grin was quite devilish this time. 'We'll stay at the pub overnight, and get an early start. It's a good sixty miles and you look whacked.' He seemed about to add something to that, changed his mind and said instead, 'Is this your brother?' nodding to where Skeet sat slumped on the platform-seat a short distance off.

'Yes, that's Skeet.'

Steve walked over, looked down at the disconsolate small form.

'Hello, sonny. What's your name?'

'Skeet Masterton.'

'No, your *real* name?'

The little boy hesitated.

'Anthony Edward Masterton.' He had to put his head right back, the man in front of him was so tall. 'I feel *sick*, mister.'

Steve, like Maddie, ignored that.

'Come on, Anthony Edward, on your feet,' he said briskly. 'The hotel's just across the street. You and your sister will feel better when you've had a wash-up and get some dinner inside you.'

Dinner! Skeet's tummy turned right over, like a porpoise in an ocean swell. His palms were clammy. He had to almost run to keep up with Maddie and the big man who strode silently through the railway building and into the street beyond.

It was a wide, tree-flanked street, almost completely deserted. They crossed it, and walked along the other pavement for a bit.

Steve Darley slowed, aware of the dragging steps behind him. When the child caught up, he asked con- versationally,

'What's Skeet short for? It's an odd sort of name.'

'I dunno.' The owner of the odd sort of name was not inclined to be helpful.

'Say I dunno — I mean, I *don't* know, *Mr. Darley* — please, Skeet,' Maddie prompted automatically.

'I dunno what it's short for, Mr. Darley,' he obliged.

'Steve will do,' said that long-legged individual, turning once more to Maddie. 'Skeet?'

'It's short for mosquito. It was a joke of Mum's, at least, that's how it started. When he was little she used to say he was as pestiferous as a mosquito, and we started calling·him Skeet for short, and it sort of stuck,' Maddie informed him.

'I see. In here, then, Skeet.' He guided them into a shabby but comfortable reception hall, put down the cases. 'Wait here a moment.'

Skeet blinked up at his sister.

'Maddie, I feel sick,' he whispered urgently.

'Not *here*, Skeet,' she pleaded, glancing uneasily at the man's broad back, across at the reception desk now. 'Not *here*. Just hang on, Skeet.'

'I can't *hang on*!' The little boy's voice rose ominously, caught the ear of the big brown long-legged·man.

Steve swung round, and acted immediately and without

43

ceremony. Skeet found himself scooped up under one arm just like the suitcases had been, and borne with complete lack of dignity, but with creditable speed, through a door at the end of the hall. Maddie, beyond humiliation, could only wait helplessly for their reappearance.

When they returned, Steve's face was unrevealing, Skeet's pea-green. The man sat the child down on a leather seat against the wall, and asked kindly,

'O.K. now, sonny?'

'O.K., mister – um – Steve.' Skeet's freckled face smiled drowsily up. He rested his head back and closed his eyes against further inquiries.

Steve Darley stood for a moment, took in the pallor, the freckles, that bright carroty hair that spiked out in all directions. Then he turned to Maddie.

'Haven't you learned by now that a travelling child shouldn't be indulged with all the sickly rubbish in creation, especially on a long, hot journey such as this one?'

Maddie blushed. Anger, pity for Skeet, and a sense of guilt made her prickle with antagonism.

'I don't need you to tell me what's best for Skeet, thank you,' she replied coldly.

'I'm telling you what's *worst* for him, not what's best. If you know it already, why indulge him?' He turned, picked up the boy. 'Come on, nipper! I'll take you to your room, and your sister can put you into bed. You'll feel like a new feller in the morning!'

Skeet gave a pale grin. His thin hands clutched at the broad, white-shirted shoulders.

'You bet, Steve!'

Maddie's lips were pressed tight together as she followed the bellboy in the wake of Steve Darley and her brother.

The room was large, shabby like the hall downstairs, but reasonably cool and comfortable. Double gauze doors opened out on to a balcony above the street. Furniture was limited to the bare necessities – a couple of chairs, a wardrobe, a marble wash-stand, and two narrow beds.

44

Steve glanced around, then down at his watch.

'I'll see you downstairs in ten minutes,' he said. 'The dining-room is on the left as you come down.'

'Thank you, I'm not hungry.' Maddie's voice was intentionally frigid.

'You'll be there, nevertheless. As I have it from Skeet, he was the only one who made free with the chocolates and lollies – isn't that so, Skeet?'

Skeet nodded agreeably. 'Maddie never ate a thing, hardly, did you, Mad? She said she couldn't look at food. Sis is always like that when she's all steamed up about something, aren't you, Maddie?'

'That's *enough*, Skeet!' She wrestled with his buttons, gave him a quelling look.

'Well, it's true,' Skeet reaffirmed, not to be quelled on any account. 'An' you *are* all steamed up – about this Yattabilla place and that man you said was so—'

'*Skeet!*' Her face was flaming. She gave him an urgent shake, none too gently, and Skeet decided that he had really better get undressed pretty quickly, since Maddie appeared to be in one of her moods.

'I'll be down presently,' she told Steve shortly. 'You needn't wait.'

'A pity! And just when the conversation was becoming so interesting!' he observed blandly. 'Very well, Madeleine, I'll leave you to it. Ten minutes, mind.'

She heard his steps retreating along the passage to a room further down the corridor somewhere. Maddie clenched her teeth. Oh, lord! Why did that wretched man have to turn up like this? And why did Skeet have to disgrace her by being sick the moment they arrived? And why, of all the people he could doubtless have chosen, had her father had to pick Steve Darley to be an executor and trustee of his estate? Not only a trustee, either, she was forced to remind herself. Maybe even a legatee, if Maddie couldn't hold out for her rights, and stay at Yattabilla for the required time!

Well, she *would* stay, she and Skeet, come what may! In

45

fact, if the man only knew, his high-handed behaviour had the effect of strengthening Maddie's determination rather than weakening it. She became more resolved than ever that nothing – and nobody! – was going to stand in her way! Sydney was behind her, and so was London and the imports firm. She had burned her boats, come all this way, and she certainly hadn't done it for nothing. Maybe Steve Darley didn't know it yet, but she could be just as determined, as single-minded, as he! She was quite fit for his scheming ways and devious charm! She wasn't in the least taken in by his motives in meeting them off the train at Noonday, either. He would doubtless do his utmost to put her off at the very start – to present Yattabilla in the worst possible light. That's why he had come to drive them there, rather than let them find their own way!

Maddie waited for Skeet to clean his teeth in the bathroom along the passage, then saw him slipped between the sheets.

' 'Night, Skeet.'

'G'night, Maddie.' His voice was drowsy, indistinct with sleepiness. 'Have a good dinner, Mad. I bet you need it, after eating practically nothing all day.'

'Thanks, Skeet, I will.' Maddie's reply was tender, in spite of herself. Mosquito, the pestiferous one, certainly did not make life any easier, but she loved him, all the same!

After making herself tidy she went downstairs, into the dining-room on the left.

Steve was already there, sitting at a table set with cheap steel cutlery. He rose when she appeared, saw her seated, handed her one of the glasses he had brought in from the bar at the rear of the hotel.

'Gin and tonic,' he informed her lazily, in answer to the unspoken query in her eye. 'I thought the ice and a lemon twist might help to cool you down – that temper, too.'

He was baiting her. Maddie glared at him repressively, and sipped her drink. It was very cold, and the lemon did give it a certain tart freshness.

'Why is this place called Noonday?' she asked, purposely ignoring that opening personal thrust. She was darned if he was going to amuse himself at her expense!

The broad shoulders in the white shirt shrugged carelessly. His sleeves were still rolled up, but Maddie noticed that he had buttoned the neck of the shirt, and now wore a neat, striped tie.

'I guess the explorer had run out of inspiration by the time he got here. He named almost every landmark after himself on the way out – mountains, gaps, rivers, creeks, even the plains. This town is sited on a permanent waterhole in the river – a stretch that never goes dry. He'd have been pretty glad to see that water-hole, with the wilga trees scattered all along it, after a long hot slog across a waterless waste, I reckon.' He quirked an eyebrow at her absorbed face. 'His diary records that he reached here at noon, and pitched camp, and Noonday it's been ever since.'

'Oh, I see.'

The train had come across that same waterless waste, too – chuffing slowly through the vibrant heat, bringing herself and Skeet with it. Maddie could realize what a welcome sight those trees and that stretch of water must have been to some weary, dry-throated, footsore discoverer of long ago. She had not yet seen the river or the trees or the layout of modern Noonday, because it had been so dark when they arrived, but her imagination was captivated, all the same.

'You think it romantic, Madeleine?' Uncanny, the way he had read her mind. 'You won't for long! You'll soon be immersed in harsh realities, my dear – and with only your stubborn little self to blame.' He ground out his cigarette, as a woman appeared from the kitchen regions, carrying two plates of mutton stew and vegetables already served out.

'No oysters tonight, I'm afraid.' Steve's grey eyes were dark with irony. 'Out here you eat what you're given, and no questions asked. And you accept the cards that a sometimes unkind Fate deals out, too, and simply do what you can with them. You'll see just what I mean before long! Salt?

47

Pepper?' He passed the cruet set, helped himself liberally after she herself had used it.

Was he warning her? Maddie glanced surreptitiously at the unrevealing mould of his weathered features. It was totally devoid of expression as he applied himself to his food.

Maddie determinedly did the same. He was trying to shake her, no doubt about that. She had thought he might do that – had almost been prepared for just these words. Even so, the little butterflies of apprehension had started fluttering alarmingly about once more inside her. She made a bid to control them, and kept her eyes fixed on her plate.

No oysters? No, and no frills, either – not out here. And all that grandeur, the Blue Balcony, the gourmet menu, the wine and music, had in any case been purely incidental so far as Steve Darley's invitation to her had been concerned. He hadn't even bothered to change for dinner, had he? Not like he had for the Greek goddess, for instance! Maddie wished that that sophisticated, proud white vision would not keep intruding into her thoughts.

It was doubtless the sight of this big, powerful, teak-skinned man, exuding self-assurance on the opposite side of the table, who was responsible for the unwelcome image her mind had conjured up unbidden.

She would never be comfortable in his company again, Maddie decided now. Not after *that*! He had been bound to realize to whom it was that his lovely companion had alluded so cattily. The only thing he didn't know was that Madeleine, too, had heard her! A pity she had not been able to catch his own murmured reply. If she had, she might have had a better chance now of knowing what he was really thinking when his eyes roved her face, and finally came to rest on her rich golden mane, just as they were doing right this minute.

'Pudding?'

Maddie shook her head.

'Cheese, then, and two coffees, please,' he told the woman

who still lingered after removing their dinner-plates. 'How long is it since your mother died, Madeleine?'

The direct question took her by surprise.

'Four years.'

'That made Skeet six, and you sixteen, is that correct?'

'Yes, that's right.'

'And you were left with the child on your hands. How did you handle it?'

Maddie's hackles rose. He made Skeet sound like an unwanted parcel, and he had never been that! He might be Skeet, and pestiferous at times, but never unwanted – *never* a burden! She wished she hadn't told Steve the mosquito bit, after all.

'I managed, thank you.' She was brief, defensive.

'How?' he persisted, but not as if it really mattered.

'Well, I – I left school and went to a business college, and took a commercial course, that's how. The digs I found were run by a nice woman who didn't mind a small boy around – she'd had a family of her own. In fact, she used to look out for Skeet when he came back from school in the afternoons, and kept him going until I could get there myself.'

The grey glance probed keenly.

'She did that for nothing? Without expectation of payment?' Steve queried, drawing the familiar cigarette papers and tobacco from his shirt pocket, and pushing his chair back a little from the table.

'Not *exactly* for nothing.' Maddie spread her fingers, and regarded them closely. 'I took on a job four nights a week,' she admitted with some reluctance. 'It was shift work in a late canteen. I used to go once I'd got Skeet to bed. They paid the waitresses quite well.'

Steve, too, was looking at her hands. Maddie put them quickly down out of sight, on her lap. They weren't really pretty hands. The nails were short and neat, because of the typing, and no amount of nightly creaming could quite disguise the fact that they had had to be useful sort of hands. Unbidden, there came to Maddie a mind-picture of other

49

hands – the slender, tapering fingers, the polished oval brightness of the Grecian goddess's beautiful nails.

'And then?'

Maddie shrugged.

'It was easier once I had a regular day-time job,' she admitted candidly.

'In an importing business, I think you said?'

'Yes, it was quite a good job, really, although without the prospect of much advancement. It was safe and secure, anyway, and I was thankful for that.' She yawned, in spite of herself. The meal, the warmth of the night, the strain of his presence, were telling on her.

Steve Darley pushed back his chair, and came round to hers.

'Come, you've had a long day. You'd better get to bed.'

His tone was kind, quite gentle, almost as though she had been a child, scarcely older than Skeet.

Maddie blushed. His hand on her elbow sent an unwelcome little shiver through her whole body. He was towering over her, and his eyes were on her hair again! Remembering made Maddie draw hastily away, rather pointedly shaking off the supporting grasp that was guiding her towards the stairs.

'Thanks' – she spoke more tartly and ungraciously than she intended – 'but I'm not so tired that I can't go up alone.'

The hand on her elbow was withdrawn abruptly, and she looked up to see that his grey eyes had fastened on her, unpleasantly. They were cold, dark, impenetrable slits, and they glittered oddly. When he spoke, his tone was at variance with those angry eyes.

'What's the matter, Madeleine?' he asked, in an amused drawl. 'Is something rattling you?'

She ignored that. All the same, her breath came quickly as she hurried up the stairs.

From the gloom at the bottom she distinctly heard a laugh – a brief, deep chuckle – but a *laugh*, nevertheless!

'Don't worry, Madeleine.' The teasing voice followed her, lifting slightly as she gained the upstairs hall, so that she would be sure to hear what it was saying. 'You needn't, you know. Cradle-snatching isn't one of my vices, and further-more, my dear girl, you don't happen to be my type.'

Maddie found that she was almost running along the cor-ridor to the room she was to share with Skeet. She somehow made herself slow down, and walk calmly, so that the man still standing in the hall below would not guess how badly her heart was behaving, thud, thud, thud, against her ribs.

For a moment, down there, she *had* been frightened – precisely why, she could not have said!

Skeet was sleeping soundly when she gained the bedroom. He had pushed away the sheet, and his small body was sprawled over, almost on to his face. There was more colour back in his cheeks, merging the freckles in with its own faint flush, but his spiky carrot mop was as unruly as ever against the pillow. In his blue striped pyjamas he looked touchingly innocent, angelic in slumber.

Maddie touched her lips fleetingly to the freckled fore-head and quietly got undressed. For a while she sat, brush-ing her hair with long, calming strokes. When she put out the light, she hesitated a moment, and then walked over to the double gauze doors, and stepped out on to the Victorian-style balcony. Its wrought-iron balustrade reminded her of something. Something painful! The Blue Balcony. It was like the Blue Balcony, except that it wasn't all picked out in blue and gilt, and beneath it there wasn't the hubbub of milling city traffic. There was just a wide, silent, tree-lined street in a dark, silent country town.

Maddie walked to the edge and peered up and down the deserted thoroughfare.

It wasn't quite deserted, after all. Across the street, almost opposite, she could glimpse a white shirt, a tall dark form. Steve Darley was leaning against a post that sup-ported the canvas awning of the shop over the way, quietly smoking a last cigarette before he, too, retired. Maddie could see the small puffs of smoke drifting lazily up towards the stars.

Cautiously she withdrew, closed the gauze doors noiselessly and slipped into bed. Lying there listening to Skeet's even breathing, she felt curiously alone, curiously depressed. It had, she knew, something to do with Steve, standing out there under the night sky.

A pity they couldn't even be friends, she thought drowsily. Not that that was possible, as things were, because they both wanted the same thing, didn't they – they both wanted Yattabilla! And anyway, hadn't he stressed just now that she wasn't his type? Not that you had to be someone's type just to be *friends* with them, did you?

Maddie lifted her head, punched her pillow, and tried once more to compose herself for sleep. She, Maddie, wasn't his type – but the Grecian goddess was. And she, Maddie, could never be like the Grecian goddess. There wasn't a hope that she *ever* could!

On which forlorn note, Maddie drifted into restless slumber.

CHAPTER FOUR

SKEET was up and dressed long before his sister next morning. When Maddie saw the empty bed beside her own, she dressed hastily, plunged the striped pyjamas and her own night things back into the canvas hold-all, and went downstairs.

No one was in evidence, although she could hear sounds of activity in the kitchen quarters.

Maddie went through the reception hall and stepped out into the street. Noonday was bigger than she had thought it to be. It was low and spreading, but with a neatness and order of planning entirely lacking in the angled jumble of thoroughfares in either London or Sydney. This was Maddie's first experience of a country town, and she was impressed by the serenity of it all – the wide straight streets, the shade trees that bordered them, and the spacious shops with their neat canvas awnings. The cars were big, modern and shiny. The gardens were colourful and luxuriant, watered from the slow-running river, the stretch that never dried up, and the dots of wilga trees were nearby.

Maddie walked a short way up the street, curious, critical. She liked what she saw of Noonday. There was no evidence of poverty or shabbiness. Every building, every car, looked as though it had a reason for being there – as if it were making its own individual contribution to Noonday's prosperity. It was a thriving, cheerful centre, sun-washed and peaceful too.

Maddie felt her own spirits lift. You couldn't help feeling good in a place like Noonday. Its modernity, its cleanliness, its tranquillity, all encouraged in her an optimism that she had not felt last night.

When she regained the hotel, Skeet was sitting on the

form by the wall looking idly over some leaflets he had got from the pile on the reception desk.

Steve was there, too. He was standing with his feet a little apart and his hands on his hips, immersed in conversation with a younger man.

When he saw her, he stopped speaking, and summoned her over with the familiar imperious gesture. It was a gesture that Maddie resented. For two pins she would have ignored it, only Skeet hadn't even looked up from his reading, and anyway, there was something undeniably attractive about Steve's companion.

He had fair, straight hair, neatly parted; smooth, youthful features in a round, congenial sort of face; happy eyes and a tan almost as deep as Steve's own. The two men were dressed very similarly, in pale, tight-legged moleskins, khaki open-necked shirts, and elastic-sided boots made of fine leather, with well-defined heels.

There, Maddie decided, the similarity ended. Steve Darley was of a more powerful build altogether, with an aura of authority which even his younger companion seemed to find slightly overwhelming, and which was probably responsible for his obvious air of deference and respect. Maddie knew just how he felt! She had an instant, common bond with this nice young man, even before they had been introduced!

'Madeleine, I'd like you to meet Tom Simson. Miss Masterton, Tom.'

Maddie found her hand grasped and wrung with refreshing enthusiasm.

'Hullo, Tom.' She smiled up into the boyishly flushed face. 'My friends call me Maddie,' she murmured invitingly, some devil inside her gloating at Steve's fleeting look of surprise.

'Do they, by Jove! Well, Maddie, I hope I'm going to be counted as one of your friends in that case,' Tom laughed. 'Thanks for getting me in on the ground floor, Steve. I reckon this one's going to set Noonday by the ears, don't

54

you? The Noonday sheilas will have to look to their laurels!'

Steve quirked a brow at her reddening cheeks, and jingled the change in his pocket impatiently.

'Tom's something of an authority on the local glamour, I believe,' he informed her smoothly. 'He's also the junior partner in our biggest Stock and Station agency – in which capacity you might enter those cast ewes for the sale next week, Tom. As I was saying, Hanson can drove them in. They'll be yarded by Thursday night for sure.'

'Yes, of course, Steve. I'll make a note.'

'Do that.' Steve's drawl was dismissing. 'Come, Madeleine. Here, Skeet, you'd better get some breakfast before we leave town.'

Tom Simson moved reluctantly to the door.

'Maybe I'll be seeing you again, Maddie, eh? Will you be coming in next week – to the sale, perhaps?'

'Madeleine won't be in at the sale, Tom.' Steve answered for her. 'She and her brother aren't staying at my place. They're going to Yattabilla.'

'To Yattabilla?' Tom was perplexed. 'Look here, Steve, you can't mean to *stay* at Yattabilla?'

'That's just what I do mean, though, Tom. Now, scram, like a good cove, while we get some breakfast – and don't forget those ewes.'

'Er – no, Steve. Well, so long, Maddie. See you.'

'See you, Tom.' Maddie couldn't keep a wistful note out of her voice. Noonday was fun! With someone like Tom, it might even have been more fun! And what would Yattabilla be like in comparison?

Tom had sounded sort of surprised that they were going out there, she and Skeet. He hadn't made it sound as if staying there would be much fun at all. Still, once there – once she was out of the masterful Steve Darley's clutches – she'd be her own boss, and do as she pleased. There was nothing to stop her coming in to Noonday any time she liked, was there? And just because Steve's sheep happened to be coming in to a sale, that didn't mean that Maddie and Skeet couldn't come, too. It was a free country, after all!

'Yes, I'll see you, Tom,' she called more loudly, more positively, and was rewarded to see the retreating figure turn and wave, quite gaily, to show that he had heard.

'Don't be too innocently impressionable, will you, Madeleine?' Steve's murmur grated on her ear as he stood aside to allow her to pass into the dining-room. 'There's a girl shortage out here, and the local lads are apt to go overboard for any imported talent that happens to show up.'

Ungallant brute! thought Maddie sorely, not even bothering to acknowledge that she had heard him. That was all he thought of her, obviously – just another girl, in a little country town where scarcity value provided almost any girl with a nice sound wicket to bat on!

Maddie remained silent through most of breakfast.

In spite of herself, her feelings were bruised. She was humiliated, for the second time in his presence. The first time, it had been the goddess. This time it had been Steve himself, quite deliberately. Just then, Maddie found herself longing to be free of his overbearing presence. It would be heavenly to say good-bye to Steve, and to be alone with Skeet once more, even if it meant being alone at Yattabilla. She longed for the moment when Steve would leave them and get out of her sight more than she had longed for anything in a good long while!

The hours dragged by. Roads, dust, and the accompanying flies were now the background to her unhappy thoughts.

Steve's big Chevvy was comfortably upholstered and well sprung, and the engine purred quietly as it ate up the miles. They were monotonous miles, and there were long spells when the shock-absorbers shook and quivered unceasingly over the deep corrugations in the dirt road.

Skeet's piping voice, where he sat in front next to Steve, rose above the muted music from the radio beneath the grille on the dashboard in an endless succession of questions.

'What are those birds, Steve?'

'The pink and grey ones? They're galahs, Skeet — a kind of parrot.'

'And those ones there? There must be hundreds of them!'

'Parakeets, Skeet. They're colourful, aren't they? They often fly around in great flocks like that. We disturbed them, and when one is disturbed, the lot take off. Noisy little beggars, eh?'

'Mm, they sure are, Steve! But pretty. What colours! I never knew there were birds like that in the world, all colours of the rainbow almost. Can you get more than one channel on that wireless?'

Long fingers flicked a switch.

'Two, actually, but this one's not got such good reception when we're travelling. Too many commercials, too.'

The switch was returned to its previous position.

'Why's there a hole in that fence, Steve — the one ahead, where the road goes through?'

'That's not a hole, young feller. Well, it is in a way, I suppose. It's a ramp instead of a gate, you see. It stops sheep and cattle getting over. Saves opening so many gates, because the car just goes over it, whereas the livestock avoid it like the plague. You'll see when we get there.'

They rattled over the sleepers on the ramp with a deafening noise that sent hundreds more of the little yellow and green birds whirring out of the gums along the fence.

'What's that, Steve? Quick, look! It — it's not a — a — *kangaroo*?' Skeet's voice was awed.

'It's a 'roo, all right, and a big feller, too. See him bounding away into the scrub. He could go faster than this car's going right now, Skeet, if he wanted to.' The man's deep voice was amused.

'Gee! Truly?'

'Dinkum, Skeet. I'm not having you on.' A pause. 'Are

57

you quite comfortable in the back there, Madeleine? If you can't see the scenery properly, three can easily fit in front, as I said earlier.'

'Thank you, I'm perfectly comfortable,' Maddie replied stiffly.

He *had* suggested that they all ride in front at the beginning of the journey, but when he had opened the passenger door and Maddie had seen that she was to be in the middle, she had hastily scrambled into the back, saying that she much preferred to stretch out.

She had a feeling, by the way that horridly expressive eyebrow lifted and the grey glint came into his eye, that Steve had not been deceived as to her motive, but he had made no further comment. He had simply opened the rear door for her as she wrestled with the handle, and saw her seated.

Now, although she could indeed stretch her legs, or even loll along the whole length of the seat if she chose, she had to admit that one could not see the scenery nearly so well from here. She had to duck her head into her shoulders to peer out at everything upon which Steve passed comment. Furthermore, the back of his crisp dark head, tanned column of neck, and wide, khaki-clad shoulders proved almost as unbearably close and provoking as if she had been sitting in the front seat, wedged between himself and Skeet!

When he pulled up in front of a gate across the road, the long trail of dust flying out behind the car caught up with them. It came flurrying into the saloon in a suffocating cloud that settled over everything and everyone.

Steve ignored it.

'Gate,' he said, in an expressionless voice.

Maddie, startled, scrabbled at the door-handle.

'*Front* passenger. Leap to it, Skeet!'

'What? Oh – sure, Steve.' The child scrambled out obligingly.

'He – he might not manage the catch, Steve. He's only little.' Maddie was defensive.

'Not too little to learn, Madeleine.' Steve's tone was hard. 'You coddle him too much.'

The child was wrestling with the gate, tugging at the upright iron bar. Steve leaned his head out of the window.

'Sideways, Skeet, not towards you. Take your time — really *look* at it, and discover how it works.' He stretched his legs clear of the pedals and started to roll himself a cigarette. Maddie hated the calmness in those brown fingers, and she hated the way he had spoken about Skeet.

The little boy was standing now on the bottom rung of the gate, working the bar this way and that in red-faced embarrassment. His carroty hair struck out in all directions, and he glanced, just once, rather despairingly, over his thin shoulders to the two people waiting in the car. Maddie just could not ignore the appeal in that glance!

'I said stay *here*.' Steve's eye had caught her movement towards the door. He leaned out the window again. 'Take your time, young nipper,' he advised Skeet once more, and one could not but admit that he sounded much more kind and patient with her brother than he had with Maddie herself! 'See what happens to the bottom of the catch when you pull the bar sideways. It releases it, doesn't it? Well, try opening the gate at the same time, Skeet, and pulling the whole thing towards you.'

The boy obeyed, and sure enough, the gate swung wide. He sent Steve a jerky wave of triumph, then stood on the bottom rung again and rode with it to its final position clear of the roadway.

'I did it, Steve!' he cried jubilantly, when the car had gone through and he had shut the gate and returned to his seat.

Steve ruffled his hair and let in the clutch.

'Sure you did, Skeet. That one'll never beat you again, eh, old cobber! Now we'll see how the next one goes presently.'

There were quite a number of other gates after that, and each time Skeet jumped out. Now he was doing it excitedly, as if the challenge of opening that gate had suddenly become enormous fun.

'That's it, Skeet.' Maddie tried to ignore the new rapport that had sprung up between the man in front and the eager boy. She tried not to feel, quite suddenly, out on the fringe. 'That's it, feller. This one is called a parrot-catch, because it's shaped just like the beak of one of those pink and grey galahs you were asking about. That bit lifts up, right? It's like a cocky's tongue, in the middle of his beak, see?'

After a time of intermittent gate sessions and long dusty stretches of road in between, they passed a fork where a notch of ironbarks separated the track into two.

Steve jerked his head to the road on the left.

'That's the way to Bibbi.'

'Bibbi?'

'Yes, my own place. It's on the other side of that ridge there.'

This time, when Maddie looked out, she could see ahead of them a long mountain range rising out of the plains in the distance. It had the pretty mauve softness lent by heat waves off the plain, but it was clear enough to see the broken line of valleys denting its horizons into deeper colour, and pale reddish escarpments, worn by the onslaught of wind and sand, made gashes in the further end, where it finally crumbled away into the plain again.

'There's Yattabilla homestead now,' Steve informed them without expression.

Maddie peered out anxiously. There was an inexplicable lump of emotion blocking her throat – a mixture of fright and longing. This was, after all, her homecoming! This was where she had been born, although she couldn't recognize a single landmark or recall a solitary feature of the surrounding terrain.

'Is *that* it?' Skeet's voice was tremulous with disappointment, disbelief. Even Maddie blinked her eyes several times, as if by doing so she could wake herself up from what she could only wish had been a dream – a nightmare!

The homestead was a dissolute dwelling of creaking timbers, whose cracks were sufficiently wide in places to render it open to the prevailing weather. (Maddie could only pray that that weather might always be kind!) One end, around which they walked now towards the verandah, was made differently from the rest. It seemed to be laced together in some way with pieces of hard mud brick.

'Pise.' That was Steve, still expressionless. 'This is the original house. The weatherboard bit was a later addition.'

Later? Maddie looked askance. How much *later* could it possibly have been? she wondered, frantically racking her brains for her scant knowledge of Australian history. It must have been one of the first habitations since Captain Cook came ashore at Botany Bay, surely!

Carefully she summoned her control, because she had a sudden hysterical desire to giggle. Somehow she managed to mask her expression and her thoughts, because Steve was watching her closely, through unrevealing, half-shut eyes.

They walked on, past the baked mud bit, to the verandah beyond. The weatherboard portion of the house was raised right off the ground, and there were wooden steps up on to the verandah. The flooring was rotten, completely gone in places.

'White ants.' The dispassionate toe of Steve's elastic-sided stockman's boot despatched a decaying piece of timber into what might once have been a garden. He placed the cases one by one on the verandah.

'So long, feller.' He patted the top of Skeet's carroty head, turned to go.

'W-won't you stay for a – well, a cup of tea?' Maddie felt somehow driven to ask.

His smile was a little grim.

'I don't think so, Madeleine, thanks. I'll leave you alone to your surprises. I'm sure that's what you'd prefer.'

'Yes – well – er—' she extended her hand— 'thank you for bringing us here. It was very kind of you to meet us in Noonday.' She was secretly enormously relieved that he was

61

going. She felt too shocked to keep up this pretence of calm much longer, and there was a lot to be said for being able to lick one's wounds in private!

'Kind?' The shrug of his broad shoulders negated her words. 'If you ask Mrs. Lawrence down there in that hut, she'll give you some tips. Lal Lawrence is your overseer, actually, but at the end of the day, he's answerable to me. Please remember that, won't you, Madeleine? And try not to keep little brother wrapped in cotton wool, will you? He's tougher than you may think.'

With a brisk and businesslike gesture of farewell, he was gone.

Maddie sat down hard on the edge of the rotting verandah and watched the dustball that was Steve's big Chevvy saloon roll slowly away, back along the road to that fork in the track that went to Bibbi.

'Gee, Maddie! It's not much of a place, is it?' Skeet's voice came disparagingly, jolting her numbed brain into action once more.

She scrambled to her feet, picked up the cases, and trod warily in the direction of what she supposed was the hall.

'Not right now, it isn't, Skeet, but let's not be too disappointed. I'll *make* it nice, you wait and see! Bring the canvas bag, Skeet, and let's go in.' Her tone was purposely bracing.

Inside was almost worse than out. It was dark and hot, with a stuffy smell of mustiness and disuse. The windows were small and Maddie found them difficult to open when she tried to do so. The catches were rusty, and the putty had worked loose from their shaky frames. The floors were wooden – cypress pine, with a pretty grain, although dull with neglect. Maddie was relieved to note that their condition was somewhat superior to that of the decaying verandahs. Some wax and her own elbow-grease might help. But that lino was beyond everything! It ran from the main hall right through to the kitchen quarters, and it was buckled and cracked and dry, breaking up altogether in numerous places. It did not take her long to realize that these were the places where the rain pelted in through the cracks in the weatherboard. It was obvious, too, from the expanse and position of the affected lino, then when it rained, a *lot* of water got in, one way and another. Maddie could only suppose that her father had either been too busy to keep mopping up the water, or else he had lost heart to the extent that he simply hadn't bothered. The water had lain there in ample pools until the heat of the atmosphere had evaporated it all again!

Maybe it did not rain all that often, anyway, Maddie opined to herself on a more cheerful note, remembering about the explorer and his hot, dry slog across the plains to Noonday, which was the only place hereabouts where the river didn't dry up. Maybe Yattabilla was a very dry place – the feed out on the plain certainly looked brown and uninteresting enough! Maybe it wouldn't rain at all – at least, not for the year she and Skeet would be here. She had read somewhere that in parts of Australia it did not rain for years and years, quite literally.

'Crikey, Mad! C'mon and look in here!' Skeet had gone before her into one of the bedrooms. 'Do we have to sleep in *here?*'

Maddie eyed the sagging, cross-legged stretchers with dismay.

Mice – or was it rats? Ugh! – had gnawed at the flock mattresses, dragging trails of kapok out on to the floor. The furniture was substantial, old-fashioned, but of good quality, under the concealing layers of dust. Cobwebs hung from the central light fitment, and in the corners of the windowpanes there were whole cemeteries of dead blowflies which had been ensnared in the spiders' cunning filaments.

Maddie swallowed – hard! He might at least have had the place cleaned up for them, mightn't he? she thought, feeling anger mounting inside her. He must have known when they were coming. Mr. Opal must have told him which train they were booked on, and that was how he had met them at

Noonday. Maybe he was as busy a man in the country as he had been in the city, and maybe there was not much time, since he could only have arrived home yesterday himself, but you'd think he might have given instructions to someone – Mrs. Lawrence, perhaps – to clean the place up, especially as Lal Lawrence was responsible to him. Maybe men just didn't think of these things, though.

Looking around her, she could well believe he would prefer to have his cup of tea when he got back to Bibbi, rather than here!

Maddie's heart hardened, and so did her resolve to stay here, come what may. It would take more than rotting boards and mouse-holes in mattresses or spiders on the window frames to drive her away from her inheritance. Steve would soon find that out!

'I'll make it nice for us, Skeet, never fear,' she vowed between clenched teeth. 'Let's see if we can find some tea or something – I'm famished, aren't you? – and then you can explore outside while I get one of the rooms ready. We'll decide which one when we've eaten, and in a day or two you shall have one of your very own.'

There was a fuel range in the kitchen, some kindling wood in the boiler-room beyond. Maddie had never seen a stove quite like this one before, but she supposed that it worked just like an ordinary fire. She got the flames crackling at last, and despatched Skeet outside to look for more wood, while she explored the cupboards.

Surprisingly, there was a healthy store of groceries laid in, all tinned, even to butter, bacon and milk. Gingerly she opened a can of bacon, found a tin of beans. By the time Skeet reappeared with an armful of firewood her face was flushed with exertion and anxiety. She had never seen tinned bacon before, but on the table she was able to set down two plates of hot beans and crisply fried rashers, and a pot of tea.

'Gee, Maddie, this is great!' She smiled at Skeet's enthusiastic pronouncement as she dug a hole in the milk-can and poured it into a jug, added the prescribed amount of water, and stirred the whole vigorously.

Darling Skeet! He was really such a dear little boy, and he had not complained again, not since that last, surprised utterance about the bedrooms. His hair stuck out in spikes that seemed every bit as excited as his facial expression. Skeet, indeed, was obviously beginning to regard the whole thing as fun! At ten years old, Maddie supposed that that was natural. You were too young to realize what was at stake, to appreciate the difficulties that lay ahead. Just now, as she looked at Skeet wolfing down those beans and the hefty chunks of tinned bacon with undaunted relish, Maddie felt as though a whole century of age and wisdom separated her from her jaunty little brother. Her shoulders felt old and stiff and heavy with the weight of the responsibility that rested there – a weight made somehow more intense because Skeet could not appreciate it, and couldn't be expected to share it.

Maddie, in fact, felt lonely.

Not only lonely – but *alone*, which was, if anything, one degree worse! As she sat there at the wooden table in the shabby kitchen at Yattabilla, she knew that she was more alone than she had ever been in her life, even though Skeet was sitting right here beside her.

After she had washed up the dishes and cleared away the remains of their meal, Maddie lit the water-boiler in the room off the kitchen, and once the water tank was hot, she set about scrubbing out the bedroom where they would sleep. That must have priority, she had decided, because Skeet by now was beginning to sound tired. The long journey was telling at last, and his voice was a little bit querulous, his laughter more shrill and strained.

Maddie recognized the signs in Skeet, and renewed the vigour of her attack on the filthy room. She ground her teeth together as she swiped determinedly at the cobwebbed windows, shut her eyes as she placed her shoe squarely on the wriggling, fat bodies of a couple of funnel-web spiders that she dislodged. The floor she left till the end. Once the boards were washed and wiped as dry as possible, she found blankets and sheets, and made up the beds, first concealing the worn mattresses in clean calico ticks which she unearthed in the linen press.

She was so exhausted by evening that the thought of preparing another meal was almost too much for her. A tin of soup, some toast, would suffice, and the inevitable pot of tea.

'Won't there be eggs, Maddie? There's hens down in the back yard there – white and ginger sort of speckled ones.'

'You'd better leave them, Skeet. They might belong to the Lawsons for all we know. You didn't actually take any eggs, did you?'

'No, but I saw some, and one of the hens wouldn't get off her nest, and she's sitting on a whole lot. I could feel them under her. She pecked my hand. See!' Skeet held out a grubby paw for inspection.

'Yes, well, maybe she's meant to be sitting on them or something, Skeet. Maybe she's been set there, to hatch out some chicks.'

'Chicks! Crikey!'

'We'll see in the morning.'

'Chicks! Golly, Maddie, I hope they're our hens and not the Lawsons, don't you?'

'We'll know in the morning, Skeet.' She tried unsuccessfully to stifle a yawn, straightened her aching back, and took him by the arm. 'Come on, darling – bed. I'm coming too.'

'Maddie, what'll we do about school? Or won't I have any? Gee, it'd be *great* not to have any school. Maybe there isn't one, and I could play with those chicks all the time – I mean, look after them just so long as they're little and don't know what to do themselves.'

'We'll find out in the morning.'

Skeet began to pull off his clothes, throwing them haphazardly in the direction of the small cane chair by his bed.

Even though one sock and his pants missed the chair altogether, and landed on the still-damp floor, Maddie felt too worn to reproach him. It was simpler, tonight, just to pick them up herself!

'Can we go into Noonday again soon, Mad? I *liked* Noonday, didn't you? It's a stupid name, but I liked the place O.K. How'll we get there, Maddie? Will Steve take us in his big car again? I can open every gate from here to Noonday now, Maddie. When can I do it again?'

'We'll see in the *morning*, Skeet. Go to sleep.'

'I'm longing for morning, aren't you, Maddie?' Skeet's voice was drowsy, but enthusiastic.

'Yes, darling,' she responded untruthfully, because she knew that that was what Skeet wanted her to say.

From her pillow, Maddie could see the ridge of hills out the window, across the plain. The ridge reared up against the night skyline, like some prehistoric monster. The clefts and scars, in profile, were like the scales on the monster's hide. The clumps of trees on the highest hill were his ears — or were they horns?

Odd to know that Bibbi was just over that ridge!

Thinking of Steve Darley made Maddie go tense in bed. Remembering those spiders, the clinging cobwebs, the mouse-holes and the dead blowflies, made Maddie remember, too, that she hated Steve. It was a pity, she mused blearily, but that was the way it was. Love for this wretched, crumbling place couldn't make her stay at Yattabilla, but hate for Steve could! That was the truth, if she really was to be honest with herself.

Maddie would have to nourish that hate, because she certainly intended to stay!

CHAPTER FIVE

IT was almost mid-morning when they woke up next day, and when Maddie went through to the kitchen, she saw that someone had left some fresh meat on the table. It was quite neatly cut up and covered over with a fine-meshed cover to protect it from the flies which were crawling over the wire, trying frustratedly to get underneath.

She brushed the flies away, took up the plate, looked helplessly at the ancient kerosene fridge which she had no idea how to work, then put the cover back on, and replaced the plate on the table. Immediately the flies increased their demented buzzing and settled on the protective gauze once more.

Maddie pressed her lips together, and walked out the door, over the shaky verandah-boards and down the steps. When she reached the little pink weatherboard cottage that Steve had pointed out, she rapped smartly on the door.

She could not pretend, even to herself, that she was taken with the woman who finally opened the door and stepped out, closing it after her in an unfriendly fashion. Mrs. Lawrence was a taciturn, grey-haired creature, with withered skin and shifty eyes. She wore a dirty cotton apron and tattered slippers.

'Well?'

'Good morning, Mrs. Lawrence. I'm Madeleine Masterton. I came down to thank you for the meat.'

'Mr. Darley said you was to be kept in meat. Lal took it up – it ain't *my* place to be waitin' on folks.'

Maddie swallowed. The woman's attitude puzzled her.

'No – er – of course not. Well, please thank Lal for me, will you? And perhaps, if he has time later, he might come up and show me how to get the refrigerator working.'

'He don't come home till sundown.'

'I don't mind how late, Mrs. Lawrence, but I must have a refrigerator that works,' Maddie replied firmly.

Mrs. Lawrence sniffed.

'You don't know much, do yer? You sure don't look much like Gerald Masterton's kid ter me.'

'Possibly I take after my mother,' suggested Maddie sweetly, but the woman's reply bested her.

'Yeah, her that cleared out on 'im. Maybe you do take after her, at that. Reckon you'll soon get sick of the life, same as what she did. You city types don't exactly fit in out 'ere, do yer?'

'Are those hens up there yours or ours, Mrs. Lawrence?' Maddie asked, deciding that the only dignified way to deal with the woman's insolence was to ignore it.

'They belong to the house. I've simply been keepin' 'em going on Mr. Darley's instructions, but you're welcome ter take over, seein' as you'll be getting the eggs. I seen yer brother out lookin' for 'em yesterday. He's not slow, is 'e, to be takin' what he don't even know is his!'

'Very well, Mrs. Lawrence.' Maddie's voice was cold. 'From now on, I shall look after the fowls, since they belong to the house. Please tell your husband that I shall expect him this evening, however late.'

She turned on her heel and retraced her steps to the homestead, aware that her legs were trembling and her palms perspiring. It would be a long time before she went down to see Mrs. Lawrence again! She could only hope that the husband, Lal, might prove a little bit more friendly and helpful.

He did, as it turned out.

When he came up that night, he was awkward, rather than taciturn like his wife – the quiet, inarticulate sort, but passably obliging. He got the fridge working, and showed her how to fill the tray and soak the wicks. He also informed her that he would bring meat to the house twice a week, and that Wednesday was mail-day. Groceries could be ordered by telephone, or she could get her own supplies if she happened to be in Noonday.

'Is there a bus, Lal, that would take me in?'

'A bus?' He scratched his head, regarded her in perplexity. 'There ain't no buses out 'ere!'

'But I can't drive a car. I don't know how to.'

He shrugged. 'Nor could she – yer ma, I mean.'

'I – I could learn,' said Maddie rather desperately.

'Yer could,' Lal agreed dubiously. 'The Buick's still in the garage, miss, but *I* ain't got time ter learn yer.'

'No, of course not, Lal. I – I'll think of something. There must be a way.' She brightened suddenly, as a new thought struck her. 'There must be some sort of school transport, Lal? Perhaps I could get a lift on that sometimes.'

Lal shook his head.

'There ain't no school transport, miss, excepting the one *in* at the beginnin' of the week, and *out* at the end.'

'In and out – to Noonday?'

'That's right, miss.' His eyes slid aware from Maddie's incredulous stare. 'Well, I better be goin' now, miss. Anything yer want, just tell my missus an' she'll pass the word.' Lal was evidently unaware of his wife's peculiar lack of co-operation! He picked up his wide-brimmed hat, clamped it on his head, and walked over to the kitchen door. There he turned. 'By the way, go easy on the electric light, will yer? The one plant's gotter do the whole set-up here, and I ain't always around the place ter be chargin' her up. Any time I'm out on the back run of the property for a coupla days, she'll run down, so keep yer lanterns handy.'

'Lanterns?'

'Yeah, the lamps, the Tilleys. Through there in the pantry.' He spat out into the darkness. 'G'night, then, miss.'

'Goodnight, Lal. And thank you for your help.'

'Any time, miss.' Maddie heard his slow steps clumping away over the hard ground outside.

She sat down in the chair beside the wooden table, and

put her head on her arms. She wanted to cry, more than anything, just then. Yes, she could wish for nothing more satisfying than to simply give way to her feelings – to sit there and sob her heart out with noisy abandon.

Instead, she got up out of the chair, and went slowly to the telephone in the hall, turned the handle with resolution, and lifted the receiver.

A woman's voice, nasally distinct, said immediately,

'Can't you hear the line's engaged?'

'Pardon?' Maddie was startled.

'Sounds like a new voice, Gladys! Who are you, dear?' asked the nasal one again.

'Madeleine Masterton, from – er – from Yattabilla.'

'Oh, I see.' The strange voice immediately became more friendly. 'You're new here, aren't you, duckie? In that case, we'll forgive you for butting in.'

'I'm sorry.' Maddie was forlorn. It seemed to her that she could do nothing right, and it was all so strange, even this present conversation. 'I didn't mean to interrupt. I just wanted the exchange.'

'Well, we won't be long, will we, Gladys, and then you can have the line. It's a party line, you see. And the rule is, listen first, and if no one's on the line, you can have it. Don't listen *in*, though. That's a different thing altogether, isn't it, Gladys?'

'Too right it is! It's the quickest way to lose your friends,' agreed the more distant Gladys.

Friends? They were something Maddie didn't have, so she couldn't very well lose them, could she?

'I'm sorry,' she repeated once more. 'I didn't mean to listen in. How do I get the exchange when the line is clear, please?'

'One long ring, and they'll answer you. You're two longs and a short if it's Yattabilla you're speaking from. The party numbers are all morse-code ones, you see. The numbers on your own line – that's our one too – can all be rung without bothering the exchange at all. You'll soon get used to it, and remember the different rings. Just latch on to your own ring for now, and only lift the receiver if it gives two longs and a short – otherwise you'll be accused of eavesdropping!'

'Yes, I see.' Maddie was contrite. 'I'm sorry I interrupted your conversation. I – I'll go away now, and come back when the line is free.'

'That's the idea,' applauded her unseen helper. 'So long for now.'

'Goodbye.'

Maddie went back to the kitchen and made herself a cup of tea to steady her frayed nerves.

A good thing Skeet was in bed and couldn't see how shaken she was! To Skeet Maddie must always see that she appeared as a tower of strength, an unshakable pillar of wisdom, through thick and thin, come what may! That was what Skeet had come to expect of her. It would never do to let him become even the tiniest bit aware of the dread and doubts that assailed his outwardly calm and confident sister!

Back at the phone, the line sounded dead. Maddie gave a single long ring, and when the voice at the other end answered, heard herself say clearly, 'Barron Creek 234D, please.'

A moment's buzzing, and then the voice she was expecting. Steve's.

'234D here.'

'Steve?'

'Is that you, Madeleine? How are you making out?' How deep, how reassuring, could be the voice of someone you *knew* – even if that someone was Stephen Gainsborough Darley.

'Quite well, thank you.' She took a breath. 'I wanted to ask you something. Is there a school nearer than Noonday – somewhere where Skeet can go?'

A pause. Then – 'I'm afraid not, Madeleine.'

Maddie sagged against the wall beside the phone. It was true, then, what Lal had told her!

'But – but how will I get Skeet in each day? So – so far?'

'I guess you'll have to do what the rest do, Madeleine. There's a perfectly comfortable hostel in Noonday, especially laid on for pupils from a distance. There's good food, supervision, and—' – his voice was dry – 'it has the added advantage of costing you nothing, not a cent! It's all on the rate-payer, for the more distant pupils.'

'But—' she was aghast – 'you can't mean – *leave* him in there? Not – not *all* the time?'

'That's just what I do mean, Madeleine. It could be very good for Skeet. He might even enjoy it, and you'd have him home each week-end,' Steve pointed out reasonably.

Home? Yattabilla, home?

'But in that case, I'll be here all alone, throughout the whole w-week.' Her voice wobbled, and tears stung her eyes. They were tears of despair. 'I w-won't even have Skeet!'

'Not losing your nerve already, are you, Madeleine?' The sarcasm in Steve's tone had a curiously astringent effect upon his listener.

'Of *course* not!' she replied vexedly. How she hated that man!

'Well then, buck up, and stop sounding like a mother doe relinquishing Bambi to the wolves. Are you still there, Madeleine?' His voice had sharpened. 'Listen, I'll come over tomorrow and we'll discuss it then.'

'That's not at all necessary, thank you, Steve.'

'I'll be there, all the same.' His deep voice was imperturbable. 'I'd prefer not to talk about it over the party line, in any case. Good night, Madeleine.'

'Good night,' she replied woodenly, then she replaced the receiver and made her way to bed.

For a long moment she stood beside Skeet's sleeping form, striving to control the panic that had set in. Yattabilla, *with* Skeet, was bad enough! Yattabilla, *without* him, would be altogether insupportable!

Maddie recalled the crisp, taunting voice of Steve Darley

73

and knew that she would have to bear the unbearable, all the same. She'd get through it somehow, even if only for the satisfaction of seeing that loathsome smugness wiped off his tanned, handsome face!

As she finally laid her head on the pillow, she thought how differently things might have turned out. If there hadn't been this legal rope binding her to Yattabilla, she could have settled in Noonday itself, and got herself a job, and Skeet could have gone to school each day in the town, and come home to her each night, like he always had.

Noonday was such a nice place – so cheerful and peaceful and prosperous, and there were friendly people there, too – people like Tom Simson, for instance. Maddie could shut her eyes and still see the warmth and admiration in his glance, the friendliness in his youthful smile. Yes! A job in Noonday, near to Tom, could have been a very pleasant way out of things. Maybe, even now, she could work Steve Darley around to the idea.

On a more optimistic note, Maddie fell asleep.

When Steve appeared in the morning he took them by surprise. Maddie had been looking out from time to time to the approach-road up which they had come in the shiny grey Chevrolet. She would watch for a rolling dust-cloud in the distance, and when she saw it, she would be able to brace herself mentally, and summon her reserves for Steve's visit. She'd need to collect her wits before that dust-cloud resolved itself into a speeding saloon with a big, brown man at the wheel.

Instead, Steve simply walked into the hall where Maddie had gone down on her knees to polish some of the dull neglect from the pretty cypress-pine flooring, and threw his hat with a deft, spinning accuracy on to the table by the telephone.

'Oh!' Maddie scrambled to her feet and wiped a sticky tendril of hair from her perspiring brow. 'It's you! I looked out just a moment ago, and there was no sign of a car.'

'I didn't come by car. I came on horseback, over the ridge.

74

It's quicker.' A keen glance raked her. 'What's the matter? You look all keyed up! Don't tell me you're nervous?'

'Should I be?' she countered, with deceptive calm. 'This meeting was your idea, not mine. I wasn't begging for company when I rang last night, if that's what you thought. I merely wanted some advice.'

'Relax, then, infant.' He grinned down at her lazily. 'I've already told you, you aren't my type, so save the intensity and maidenly fluttering for someone young and impressionable.' He sat down, stretched long legs in dust-covered riding-boots, and reached for tobacco and papers in his shirt pocket. 'I'll have some tea if it's on the go, Madeleine – or could you possibly run to a beer?'

'No, I could not!' she replied tartly. 'If you wait there, I'll bring tea,' she added repressively, and marched off to the kitchen, irritated beyond measure. Steve got under her skin at every turn! She had a feeling that he did it on purpose, too – part of the 'get-her-out-of-Yattabilla' campaign? If so, he'd be disappointed.

'Where's Skeet?' he asked, when she came back with the tea.

'I sent him down to play at the creek. I thought it better that he wasn't around while his schooling is being discussed. It – it might make him feel insecure.'

Steve eyed her over the rim of his tea-cup.

'There's not much chance of his feeling insecure if you handle it right. Kids like to be the same as other kids, Madeleine. Surely you've found that out by now? You might even remember it from your own childhood days – they weren't all that long ago!'

'What do you mean?'

He shrugged carelessly.

'Either he stays out here with you and gets his schooling by post or some other, more unsatisfactory means; or he goes into Noonday during the week, and feels himself to be one of the crowd, doing the same as they do. It's easy to guess which Skeet would prefer, if he could look at it objectively, without those sisterly but misguided little hands of yours playing jigsaws with his emotions all the time, so he doesn't know where he is.'

'How dare you!' Maddie was incensed. 'Are you suggesting that I won't do what's best for Skeet? That I'd put my own feelings before his welfare?'

Steve drew on his cigarette and regarded her through critical grey eyes.

'You said it – I didn't,' he answered calmly. 'If you want to prove your point, you'll let him go to the hostel in Noonday, just like all the other boarders, and he can come out at the week-ends, just like they do too. It'll be the first taste of normality that he's had in his life for a while, I dare say.'

Maddie bit her lip and dropped her eyes to her hands, which were clenched tightly in her lap.

'It's what I intended to do, in any case,' she stated coldly, because she knew she was cornered. She ran her tongue over her dry lips, and tried to coax some friendliness back into her voice. 'Steve, there really isn't any reason why I couldn't stay in Noonday, too, is there, and come out at week-ends with Skeet? What I mean is – well, Yattabilla, Noonday – it amounts to almost the same thing, doesn't it?'

He laughed softly. To Maddie it was a thoroughly unpleasant sound.

'So you *are* losing your nerve! I thought as much! Or is it that you can't face the thought of not possessing your little brother for a whole seven days out of every seven? No, Madeleine, it is *not* the same thing. As you say, it's almost the same, but not quite, and the letter of the law is inflexible where definitions of this particular nature are concerned. You either stay at Yattabilla, or you don't.'

'But—' Maddie's eyes had filled with tears of sheer frustration – 'But my father didn't know about Skeet when he made that stipulation,' she pleaded.

'But *you* knew about him when you accepted it, didn't you?' Steve pointed out with characteristic ruthlessness. 'Legally, I'm afraid that Skeet doesn't exist – not as

Gerald's son. We've checked the birth register in the district in London where he was born, and the paternity side is unfortunately a blank. Whether your mother was too bitter even to write Gerald's name, or whether she was simply distraught, is anybody's guess, but there's no doubt that it was hardly fair to Skeet.'

Maddie opened her mouth to speak, but Steve's raised hand called for silence, so she closed it again.

'There is no doubt,' he went on, 'that Skeet is Gerald's child, please understand that. But legally – no.'

'Oh-h.' Maddie's eyes were round with hurt.

Steve shifted his weight in the chair. He too, looked grave – unhappy, almost, Maddie would have said as she found herself trying to analyse his expression.

'Look, Madeleine' – he leaned forward, towards her, persuasively – 'why not be honest with yourself and with me, and admit that Yattabilla isn't what you thought it was going to be, and that you aren't prepared to see it through on Gerald's terms. I'll drive you back to town in time for the evening train, and you can talk to old Opal, and try to contest the will.'

Yes, that would no doubt suit *him* all right, thought Maddie bitterly to herself.

She pushed back her chair with an oddly final gesture.

'Thank you for your suggestions,' she said wearily, 'but if this is the only legal way, then I shall take the only way that's open to me. After all,' she couldn't resist adding acidly, 'if the law is as inflexible as you say, there would be little point in contesting it anyway. I shouldn't have expected any helpful advice from the other involved party, in that case.'

She rose from the chair, and Steve got to his feet too. He seemed put out. Not just put out, but really angry for the very first time, and she knew that she had flicked him on the raw with that last remark. Maybe he realized that his chances of getting Yattabilla weren't quite so bright as he had anticipated, in spite of the spiders and the blowflies and the worn, mouse-eaten mattresses, and the white ants in the timber.

Steve cursed softly. The next moment Maddie's shoulders were grasped in a hard hold. His hands were cruel, bruising the soft flesh under her shirt. There was a stormy glitter in his eyes as he looked down at her, and he even had the nerve to give her a fierce, brutal shake.

'Listen to me, Madeleine, and stop talking like that!' he told her on an oddly harsh, rough note. 'Why can't you be sensible about the whole thing? God, do you think a man *likes* to go through what you're putting me through? Do you think it's pleasant for me to go on just as I always do, over there at Bibbi, over that ridge, with every modern comfort, every convenience, a plane, a car, a swimming-pool, an air-cooling system – the lot – while you and Skeet sweat it out in this hell-hole of rot and filth and—'

'Don't tell me your conscience bothers you?' Maddie interrupted sarcastically.

'Enough of that, Madeleine!' he barked, so forbiddingly that she experienced a pang of pure fright. His expression told her that she just might have gone too far! 'You know perfectly well what I mean. You're city reared, even if you are Gerald Masterton's daughter. You're just a foolish, misguided, stubborn child, and—'

'And not your type,' she finished for him, gazing pointedly at his hands on her shoulder. 'Thank you,' she continued, as he let her go and reached for his hat. 'It's more than kind of you to be concerned, but I think you'll agree it's pointless to continue this discussion. We see things from precisely opposite angles. It's natural in the circumstances, wouldn't you say?'

Steve rammed his hat on his head, glared down at her furiously.

'And what in tarnation is that remark supposed to mean?' he demanded angrily.

'I'll leave you to figure it out on your way back over the ridge,' she replied demurely.

'The hell you will!'

With a look that should have put her under the decaying floorboards upon which she stood he turned on his heel, and clattered down the steps without a backward glance. It was obvious that Steve Darley was a very angry man indeed!

Maddie felt a satisfying spurt of triumph as she gathered together the empty cups and put them on the tray. She had won that round, no doubt about it!

She hummed a little tune to herself on the way back to the kitchen, there to be pulled up short by the sight of Steve once more. This time he was to be seen out the window, sitting long-legged in the saddle on a restive and powerful bay stallion. He was leaning out of the saddle, actually, and talking down to Mrs. Lawrence, who, still in her dirty apron and the carpet-slippers she always wore, was standing with a kitten wriggling in her arms. She must have been out looking for it as Steve was leaving.

Maddie put down the tray, and crept to the window, listening unashamedly to see if she might hear what they were saying.

'—everything in the house when she arrived?' That was the end of a question from Steve.

'Yes, Mr. Darley, I left it like you said. Lal took up some meat, like you said, too. Everything was just the way you ordered.'

'Right, Mrs. Lawrence. I'll see Lal on my way out just now.'

He turned the stallion's head, and minutes later the horse and man were cantering easily away towards the ridge. With his broad-brimmed hat pulled well down over his eyes and his lean body slanted to the stallion's gait, Steve Darley appeared rakish and satisfied, as if he hadn't a care in the whole wide world. He didn't look at all like a man who had just been vanquished!

Maddie suspected – *more* than suspected – that her victory had been a hollow one, after all!

She sat down in one of the rickety kitchen chairs. Just

79

imagine! If she hadn't happened to come through just now, and overheard that tiny snippet of conversation, she might never have known that Steve Darley had actually *arranged* the homecoming she had got, in advance.

The filth, the spiders and cobwebs, the dusty mattresses and unmade beds with the kapok tumbling through the springs (ugh!) – they had all been left like that on purpose. They were all part of the Discouragement Committee, and Steve had actually stooped to connivance with that dreadful Mrs. Lawrence, so that Maddie would get precisely the reception that she had!

Maddie blinked in bewilderment and hurt. There were tears in her eyes, but she was hardly aware that she was brushing them away with the back of her hand before they could spill over. She felt dazed with disillusionment. She had known he was ruthless, yes. You could see a mile off that he was the sort of man who would let nothing stand in his way. But to sink to such deception as this! To stoop to this level! Maddie could hardly believe it, and yet what else was there to believe? She had heard it with her own ears – 'I left it like you said, everything was just the way you ordered.'

Oh, *Steve*!

Maddie supposed that this was one of the most painful lessons a human being could ever experience – the discovery that someone you had liked (well, not *liked*, not a bit, really – respected, that was the word) could do you down, and stab you in the back when you were not even looking.

She couldn't ever trust him after this, she realized sadly. All those things he had said about feeling bad because she was here in this awful house and he was over the ridge in his lovely modern one – they meant absolutely nothing, not a thing! They were just a blind.

Maddie scrubbed at her eyes with her knuckles. A righteous anger was beginning to supplant the hurt and disillusion. She would show him! She certainly would! And if 'showing him' meant that she had to live at Yattabilla alone, without Skeet, for five whole days in every week, well, she could do that, too! The time would soon pass. She would keep herself extra busy on those days, and at night she would make her mind an absolute blank, so that it would not dwell on the absence of her little brother's even breathing and comforting presence in the next room, or on the strange creaking sounds that the verandah boards made as they contracted in the evening air after the heat of the day. Sometimes, when they groaned in the darkness, it was almost as if someone, or something, was pressing them down with a stealthy tread. Someone such as a tramp, or a – well, a bushranger, if they still had those in Australia. Something such as a wombat or one of those big kangaroos like the one that had bounded along beside Steve's car, or maybe even a snake. Maddie decided that she wouldn't be very frightened if it turned out to be a wombat noise or a kangaroo noise – but a snake? Ooh! Her slender shoulders shook at the mere idea.

Stupid! she chided herself. She must not let her imagination get out of hand.

Maddie took a grip on herself, and went into the boiler-room for some potatoes which someone – Lal, presumably – had dug up and put in a dented kerosene tin which served as a pail. She wondered where they had come from. Certainly not from the 'front garden', where weeds were rampant, and the only recognizable surviving flowers were a few struggling geraniums and some sort of broad-leafed thing which she supposed might be a canna. More probably they had come from the plot down near the fowl-yard, where she had recognized the spindly remains of dying artichoke tops and a wandering patch of melons.

When Skeet came in, she had peeled the potatoes and put them to boil on the big black stove. She had decided that she would form them into cakes, and serve them with some more of the tinned bacon. Maddie was not quite sure what to do with the meat that Lal had left, and she was still far too upset by Steve's visit, with all its implications, to be bothered pondering over cuts of mutton just now.

Skeet was dirty. His face was covered with dust, and there were pieces of straw in his hair.

He returned her stare of disapproval with an undaunted grin.

'I've been down at the hen, Maddie – the one on the eggs. I'm sure we're going to get chicks!' He rubbed a sweaty palm over his forehead, leaving a grimy trail in the dust already there. 'Gee, Mad, I wonder how long it'll be before we get them?'

'We might not, Skeet,' she warned cautiously. 'They might not be even fertile.'

'Fertile?'

'Yes. You know, the right sort of eggs – ones with little chicken seeds in them.'

He gave her a withering look.

'Don't be silly, Maddie. Of course they'll be the right sort. She wouldn't be sitting on them all this time if they weren't, would she? *She's* not silly! She's a very sensible hen, she even knows me now when I lie down beside her to look underneath. She doesn't even peck me any more, 'cos I've tamed her. Of course she'll know about the chickens. Hens just *do*!'

'Well, I hope so, Skeet.' Maddie's ignorance of poultry was only slightly less abysmal than her brother's. She remained unconvinced, but secretly hoped that he might be right. Chickens would be fun! They would help her to pass the time when Skeet was away in Noonday at school.

Maddie felt a hollowness inside her. She would have to tell Skeet soon. It was no use putting it off. She opened her mouth, and found herself asking instead,

'What are you doing?'

Skeet, quite obviously, was scratching. Even as she watched, his efforts became more frantic, and tiny red blotches appeared on his neck and throat, on his bare arms and legs.

'Oooo – oh!'

Maddie pulled him over to the window to inspect him

more closely.

'Why, Skeet, it's fleas or something. Little tiny red things. You're smothered in them!'

'So's Etta, but *she* doesn't seem to mind.' The little boy's voice was muffled as he twisted around in an effort to reach his back.

'Etta? Who's Etta?'

'Henrietta. My hen. I call her Etta for short. She's got them too, but they don't seem to bite her like they do me. Ow!'

'That's it, Skeet, that's what they are – hen fleas. I don't think they live long, but–' she watched his ineffectual scratching for only a moment– 'you'd better have a bath, and a complete change of clothes. Come on, quickly!'

Maddie drew the pan of potatoes to one side of the stove, and marched him off in the direction of the bathroom.

Skeet, for once, did not protest, although normally he hated baths. Over the sound of the running water, Maddie told him that he must not go near the hen again.

The little boy lowered himself into the bath and looked at her mutinously.

'Well, not quite so near,' she amended, weakening at the sight of his forlorn expression and blotched body as he began to soap himself.

'No, not quite so near,' Skeet hastened to agree.

'You might frighten her off the eggs, anyway, Skeet, and then you'd be sorry.'

'Look, Maddie, haven't I told you, Etta an' me are *friends*. Anyway, she doesn't scare easy.'

'Maybe not. but the chicks will.'

'No, they won't. And she'll be walking about when they come, Maddie, not sitting for ever in that musty old hay. That's where the fleas are – in the straw. When the chicks come, we'll all go walking about together, and the fleas won't get me then.'

Skeet stepped out of the bath and began towelling himself.

Maddie swallowed. Then she made herself say what she knew had to be said.

'At the week-ends, Skeet. You can walk around with them at the week-ends only.'

'How d'you mean, Maddie?' The towel was arrested in mid-air.

Carefully she explained about the school. She told him about the bus in at the beginning of the week, and the one out on Fridays, about sleeping at the hostel and playing with a lot of other children.

To her surprise – her chagrin? – Skeet accepted all she had told him with equanimity, almost, in fact, with actual enthusiasm.

'In Noonday? Truly? That'll be great. How many of us will there be on the bus? What time will it come?'

'I don't know, Skeet. I'll have to find that out.'

'I like Noonday, don't you? I reckon I'm really glad the school's in Noonday. Can you come too, Maddie?'

She shook her head.

'No, darling, I'm afraid not, but you'll have lots of play-mates, so you won't really miss me. I'll have to look after the house here, you see. Someone will have to mind Yatta-billa.'

'Yes, and Etta, too. Someone'll need to keep an eye on Etta, and it can't be me, not when I'm in Noonday. I'd rather it was you than Mrs. Lawrence, anyway, Maddie. I don't think she likes hens, do you?'

Maddie bit her lips as she patted calomine lotion on to Skeet's blotches. So much for her own misgivings! And so much for the loyalties of extreme youth! Skeet wasn't even going to *miss* her – not in the way she was going to miss him, at any rate! Why, he was going to miss Henrietta more than Maddie! He was going to miss a hen more than his very own sister. It hadn't even occurred to him how lonely and de-prived Maddie was going to feel, all by herself here without him.

Steve's recent words rang in her ears like a jibe—

'It's easy to guess which Skeet would prefer—'

Skeet's thin shoulders shifted under her grasp.

'Ow, Maddie! Don't do it so hard.'

Maddie came out of her trance to find that her fingers were indeed digging into Skeet's arm. Even the savage little jabs with which she found herself applying the pad of cotton-wool to the blotches were quite foreign to her gentle nature.

'Sorry, darling.' Maddie hugged Skeet in compunction.

What was that Darley man doing to her? she wondered, as she bent to pick up the damp towel. She mustn't let him get her down like this. She might have to live at Yattabilla with Steve as a neighbour, but she was darned if she was going to let him have any further influence in their lives after this!

Maddie's cheeks were flushed and angry, and when she returned to the kitchen, she found herself wielding the potato-masher with every bit as much energy and indignation as she had that pad of cotton-wool!

CHAPTER SIX

MADDIE felt like crying when she waved Skeet off on the bus on Monday morning. She could not even hug him or anything like that, because of the other passengers in the dusty vehicle.

Three other boys and two little girls, all in clean cotton clothes, all with country-brown, inquisitive faces, leaned out the long back window to get a better look at the new pupil as he gave a jaunty wave and strutted independently towards the waiting bus, clutching his small suitcase.

The driver, an elderly man with a mop of grizzled hair and leathery jaws studded with grey bristles, swung down the steps and shoved Skeet inside.

'Grab the hand-rail, that's it, sonny.' He turned for a second before pulling the door shut behind him. 'He'll be O.K., miss, you betcher he will! Siddown, you lot at the back, and get away from that winder – that's if yer don't want ter come a cropper on the ground out there!' The driver slid a conspiratorial grin in Maddie's direction as he added, 'Maybe you *do*, though, eh? Maybe you'd all *like* it if I was to take yer to the 'orspital instead of the school, eh?'

'Yes! Yes!' chorused the children, giggling delightedly.

Maddie made herself smile. It seemed to take a long time for the bus to jerk away down the road, and her lips were stiff with the effort of keeping up that smile. She felt as if she had lost Skeet – really *lost* him!

All day she fought against the swamping tide of loneliness that engulfed her, but with little success. There did not seem much point in doing anything without Skeet. It wasn't even worth making proper meals without his eager little presence at the table. Maddie eyed the stack of fresh meat which Lal had brought in disgust. How could one person possibly get through that? How, indeed, could one person even be bothered to cook it!

At night the loneliness got worse. Not only were there all the snuffling, sighing night noises to identify, the groaning verandah boards to analyse, there was also this consuming anxiety for Skeet. How strange he must be feeling! Maybe even frightened. He had never slept away from home before, and he wasn't used to country people and country towns, even if he had liked Noonday when he was there with Maddie. He was not used to discipline, either – not really – especially the discipline of a boarding hostel. They would have to be strict, Maddie was sure, because there would be so many children there all at once, and Skeet wasn't really accustomed to strictness. He would not cry, she didn't think. Skeet was good at being brave, at 'not crying'. But he might *feel* like crying, and that would be awful!

Maddie turned her head into her pillow, and cried *for* him. She cried for the little brother she had tended and protected, the little boy who wasn't legally there at all, the little baby whose paternity had not even been stated on his registration form. And then she cried for herself – for the lonely, frightened girl she knew she was. When she opened her eyes and looked through her fingers out of the window into the dark, her tears made the prehistoric monster silhouetted on the ridge all wavery and strange. He looked as if his long, valley-scarred body was shaking with amusement.

The monster was laughing at her plight, and Steve Darley, over the ridge there at Bibbi, would be laughing, too!

Somehow she worked her way woodenly through the next day.

That night she had company, of a sort that Maddie would have preferred not to have at all. She was getting ready for bed when something made her glance out on to the verandah and there it was. A snake! Maddie had to blink her eyes twice to be sure, and even in that moment it began to slide silently away across the boards and over the edge of the verandah itself. The strangest part, for Maddie, was that its passage was utterly noiseless. Not a single creak from the rotting timbers gave away its presence.

Maddie made for the telephone in blind panic, hardly pausing to check that the line was free.

'B-Barron Creek 234D? S-Steve?'

'Madeleine? Is that you?' His voice sounded comfortingly close, gruff with surprise.

'Steve, there's a – a snake.' Her own voice trembled, trailed off into nothingness. The relief of hearing him seemed to have rendered her temporarily speechless.

'Did it get you?' he asked in an odd, abrupt sort of way. Then, more harshly. 'Madeleine, answer me! Were you bitten?'

'N-no,' she whispered. 'I'm all right.'

'No harm done, then. Mind you, even if you had been, they've a comprehensive anti-venene now, you know.' Steve's tone had altered subtly. There was almost a teasing note in it, she could swear. 'It does for all types, which is handy, since one sometimes doesn't get a chance to identify them properly.'

'You mean they can b-bite you without you even *seeing* them?' Her question was at treble pitch.

'Don't be silly, Madeleine. I didn't say that at all! Where's this one now?'

'It's g-gone. It slid over the end of the verandah.' Heavens above! He couldn't think that she would be standing here carrying on a phone conversation with that snake still around, surely?

'What colour was it? Did you get a good look?'

'B-black. It was black.'

'Sure?'

'Of course I'm sure! It was black and horrible. Sort of *sinister*.'

Steve laughed. He actually laughed – outright!

'Not to worry, Madeleine. The black ones aren't sinister at all. It might have made you feel rather off-colour if it had bitten you, but that's about all, so cheer up! And remember, the poor brute's a lot more scared of you than you might think. All he wants to do, nine times out of ten, is to get out of your way. What you have to watch is that you don't tread on one by mistake.' Silence. 'Do you follow me, Madeleine? Snakes have not got very good eyesight, as it happens, and they might not see you until you're almost upon them. They go by vibrations more than actual sight, so it's a fair bet that you'd spot them before they spot you. If you don't, you can be unlucky.' There was dry amusement in Steve's drawling voice.

'Unlucky! I think you – you're heartless!' Maddie mumbled.

'What did you say, Madeleine?'

'Nothing,' she retorted crisply. 'I'm sorry I bothered you over such a minor matter.'

Steve chuckled. 'No bother, I assure you,' was his bland reply. 'Any time at all, in fact. I enjoy these little chats in the middle of the night.'

'You – oh!'

'Just one thing, though, Madeleine – and I'm being serious now – phone me promptly and speak a little more distinctly if one ever happens to get holed up inside the house, will you, there's a good girl?'

'Holed *up*?'

'Yes, holed up. Snakes don't care much for being cornered, you see. If they think their freedom is at stake, they're apt to get a bit – er – aggressive. So phone me without delay if it ever happens, won't you?'

Maddie found herself struggling for words.

'Won't you, Madeleine?' Steve's voice was insistent over the wire.

'No, I won't. I'll never phone you again, Stephen Darley, that's the one thing you may be sure of. I wouldn't phone you again if you were the last man on earth! Not even if there were f-fifty snakes holed up in this house! Not even if there were kangaroos and c-crocodiles as well!'

She slammed the receiver down right in the middle of his rich, deep chuckle. She was so furious that she had to restrain herself from actually tearing the phone off the wall. One could hardly blame the instrument, though, for that unfeeling creature at Barron Creek 234D!

Maddie was still seething with indignation as she clambered into bed. Not once did her thoughts turn snakewards again, and surprisingly, she slept almost immediately.

When Lal came up to the house in the morning, Maddie asked him about the car. She had wanted to ask him for days now, but he was always rather taciturn, and came and went with scarcely a word. She had decided that Lal was essentially a man of action, because although he was so grudging with actual speech, whenever she asked him to do anything for her, he was quietly obliging. In manual activity, he was happy enough. Socially, he just couldn't be bothered. If she remarked that it was a nice morning, all she was likely to receive was a grunt of assent. A trite observation about the heat merited a similar acknowledgement, and already she had given up trying to make light conversation to Lal.

Every time she passed the Buick sitting in the garage, it presented a challenge to Maddie. What a boon it would be if only she could drive! How it would improve her present state of dependence on Steve for almost everything! Why, she could even drive into Noonday sometimes, and see Skeet during the week. Maybe she would even get to know Tom and some of the other young people of her own age in the town.

The more she pondered over it, the more it seemed almost essential that she should learn to drive that car, especially if she was to be here, virtually in solitary confinement, for a whole year. That thought gave Maddie the incentive to mention it to Lal.

'Can you drive, Lal?'

The man scratched his head uncertainly.

'I ain't got a licence to, if that's what yer mean,' he replied.

'No, but do you know how to drive? Could you teach me? Give me some lessons in the Buick?'

'Lessons!' Lal looked askance. 'Stone the flippin' crows, miss! As if I got the time ter be givin' sheilas drivin' lessons! I got me work ter do.'

'Not sheilas, Lal, just one sheila. Me. Couldn't you, Lal, please? Just sometimes, now and then?' Maddie persuaded.

Lal, however, was adamant.

'No, I rakin' well couldn't. What d'yer think Mr. Darley'd do if I was ter leave off me work ter give drivin' lessons? 'E'd give me the boot, that's what. E's me boss, miss, and I'm answerable to 'im, don't forget.'

Maddie had temporarily overlooked that fact, she had to admit. She turned away in defeat.

'Anyway, the battery'll be flat an' everythink after all this time,' Lal observed dourly as he went down the verandah steps.

'Maybe I could teach myself, if you could get it right for me, Lal?'

'Maybe yer could, at that, if you was ter get one of them drivin' manuals or somethink. There's plenty of bleedin' space for beginners out 'ere, anyway.' Lal gave a brief guffaw at his own joke, and lumbered off.

His parting remark set Maddie thinking all over again. There *was* plenty of space around out here for learners. Perhaps she could indeed teach herself, with the aid of a book and a new battery. To get those, she would have to get into town somehow, into Noonday.

It was then that she remembered the sale. It must be on Friday, mustn't it, because Steve had said his sheep would be in the yards on Thursday night. If only she could get into Noonday on Friday, she and Skeet might be able to come home together. That bus-driver had seemed a kind, friendly sort of man.

Maddie tackled Lal once again. Did he, by any chance, know how she could get into Noonday on Friday, short of walking? Was there anyone who might take her with him? Someone he knew who would be going to that sale, for instance?

Lal scratched his head again, and finally came up with the obvious reply – the one Maddie had overlooked!

'Reckon Mr. Darley might take you in, if you arst 'im.'

'Anyone *except* Mr. Darley,' she amended hastily.

'Anyone *except* Mr. Darley?' echoed Lal, eyeing her firm expression in some puzzlement. 'Well, let's see now. There's a stock lorry comin' in with a load of weaners from over at Barron Downs. I reckon she'll be passin' the twin-fork to Bibbi soon after sun-up, if that's any use ter you.'

'Soon after sun-up?' Maddie found herself beaming up into Lal's brooding face. 'The very thing, Lal! Thank you! I'll try it.'

Lal nodded.

'Ted Widmore's the cove who's bringing' 'em in. 'E's a contractor for that sort of thing, but 'e's a decent bloke, Ted.' He spat neatly into the 'front' jungle that had once been a garden, and walked away.

Maddie spent the better part of Thursday evening preparing for her trip to Noonday. She washed her hair and whitened her best shoes, and pressed her cotton two-piece. It was of straw-coloured material, with a white collar, and might have appeared drab on lots of girls, but Maddie had chosen it because not only was it well within her price range, but the neutral shade was a perfect foil for her pale complexion and golden hair. With it she would wear brief white nylon gloves. She did not possess a hat.

When she was getting ready, she kept her excitement in check by reminding herself that she might not get a lift at all. 'Soon after sun-up' was a fairly vague attempt on Lal's part to pinpoint the precise time when the lorry might pass. It could be an hour either way, and she would have to walk to the twin-fork first. That must be a good two miles up the road, and would take her at least half an hour, maybe even an hour. She had better leave the house while it was still dark, to give herself a better chance of intercepting Ted Widmore. If transport was his business, then he probably would not mind transporting a girl along with his weaners, whatever *they* might be.

There was a welcome rustle of cool air amongst the gum-leaves when Maddie slipped out of the homestead next morning. Only the palest mirror of colour showed her where the eastern sky was. Down at the creek the frogs were still croaking harshly, the high, persistent song of the little green one interrupted every now and then by the sudden, base 'gerrup' of a big mud-coloured daddy toad. His deep voice would silence the trilling choir for half a minute at a time, and then the chorus would begin all over again.

Maddie was wearing her canvas casuals on her feet, and in her hold-all she had put her good white shoes, so that they would be clean and smart to slip on as she and Ted Widmore and the weaners were approaching the town. If the frogs could sing, so could she! It was a morning for singing, Maddie decided, because it was the morning she was going into Noonday – at least, she hoped she was! She must not let her pace slacken, because the mirror in the sky was spreading into a flame and rose-coloured dawn, and she must reach the turn-off to Bibbi by sun-up.

She waited there for perhaps half an hour, sitting on a log and admiring the changing hues as the sun crept up the horizon. Then she heard the grinding noise of a heavy vehicle's approach. When it was quite near, she waved it down, and was gratified to hear the driver change down his gear and finally stop right beside her.

The rest was easy.

After a swift, appreciative inspection, Ted Widmore said, 'Well, I'm jiggered!' and then he said simply, 'Hop up,' and opened the passengerside door for her. He even put out a large rough hand to haul her up on to the running-board, from where she was able to slide into the seat at his side.

'A beaut day, eh?'

'Yes, beaut!' Maddie agreed enthusiastically.

93

Everything was beaut, because she had managed to hitch a lift into Noonday after all, and when she returned to Yattabilla in the evening she meant to have a driving manual, and a battery for the Buick, and then she would teach herself how to drive that car. Maybe, very soon, she would be able to get into Noonday and back to Yattabilla under her very own steam. The idea appealed to Maddie enormously!

She chattered away to her companion, glad that she had kept her old canvas shoes on when each gate came along and she had to jump down into the dust to become the gate-opener. When Noonday came into sight, spreadeagled over the plain beside the brown water-hole with the wilga trees nearby, she put the canvas shoes into the hold-all and slipped on the white ones. Then she pulled on her neat white gloves.

Ted watched these operations with interest, one eye on the track and the other on his unexpected hitch-hiker. It wasn't every day he struck it lucky this way – and to get the gates opened, too—

'I'll drop you in the main street, Maddie, if that's O.K.? There is really only one main one, so you can't get bushed. The shops are mostly down this end, see?'

'Thanks, Ted – and thanks again for the lift.' Maddie jumped down and pushed the door shut. 'Where do you go from here?' she called up to Ted.

He jerked his head in the direction of a line of tin-roofed buildings.

'Over there. That's the sale-yards. Sheep first, cattle after. Well – ' a grin – 'so long, Maddie. Do it again some time, will you? Any time at all's O.K. by me!'

'Yes, I will, Ted. Goodbye.'

She hoped she wouldn't have to, though, not again. Because, next time, she hoped she'd be driving herself. That way, she would not have to ask Lal if he knew of anyone passing, and neither would she have to ask Ted, although he certainly had not seemed to mind, but had been genuinely

94

glad to have her company. Most important of all, she would not have to ask Steve. She never intended to ask Steve anything, ever again – not anything at all!

Preoccupied, Maddie turned and cannoned straight into the object of her thoughts.

'Oh!'

Steve steadied her, and lifted his hat.

'Good morning, Madeleine. You seem to make a habit of trying to knock a chap over – one way and another.' His voice was dry, but his grey eyes were alight with amusement. Then he frowned. 'Where's your hat?'

'I haven't got one,' she replied defensively, nettled that he had hardly spared a glance for her pretty biscuit two-piece and neat white gloves. Just because he was sporting one of those rather battered, broad-brimmed stockman's affairs, he needn't make her own lack of a hat sound such a crime, need he!

'Then you get one right now,' she was told. 'You can put it down to the Yattabilla account. In fact, that's something I've been meaning to speak to you about, Madeleine. I hope you'll use that account for any necessities at all, quite apart from groceries and household goods. Don't go short of anything through stupid pride, will you? You're quite fit for it, in my opinion! Just remember that it's not to me that you'll be beholden, but to your own father's estate. In other words, it's no more than your due.'

Maddie, for some reason, was touched – not by what Steve had actually said, but rather by the way in which he had said it. His voice was kind, and even his eyes had become gentle and smiley as he looked down into her own upraised face.

'Thank you, Steve. I'll get a hat, I promise.'

'That's it! And always wear one, Madeleine. Every time you go outside, even at Yattabilla, be sure to have your hat with you. The Australian sun can be cruel as hell to your sort of fair English complexion.'

'Yes, Steve.' Maddie's voice was submissive. She had not

thought he had even noticed her creamy skin. Maybe the man was human, after all! A dimple grooved her cheeks at that, and she peeped up to see if the human side was still in evidence. It wasn't!

'How did you come into town, Madeleine?'

Maddie told him about hitching a lift with Ted Widmore, and as she told him Steve's scowl got fiercer and fiercer.

'I don't want you doing such a thing again, do you hear! It's most unsuitable, and you took a heck of a risk. Ted's a decent cove, it's not that, but it could have been *anyone* coming along an outback road at that hour. It's hardly the way for Gerald Masterton's daughter to get around, anyway, is it? You should have rung me, and I'd have brought you myself.'

'The last time I rang you,' Maddie could not resist pointing out, 'you were hardly sympathetic!'

'What? Oh! You mean about the snake?' Steve had the nerve to grin at the memory. 'Touché, Madeleine. I'm sorry about that, but I was too far away to be of concrete assistance, and it was the only way to handle it. You'd had a fright, and were badly in need of bracing up. There's nothing like a spot of healthy indignation to put fear to flight, eh? Aren't I right?'

'Well—' Maddie gave an answering, reluctant smile, in spite of herself.

'Let's call it quits for now. You go and get that hat, and in return I'll promise to be more sympathetic next time! O.K.?'

'Yes, Steve, O.K.'

He touched his brim in a gesture of farewell, and strode off. Maddie watched him cross the street and walk in the direction of the tin-roofed sheds that Ted had pointed out. She watched until he had disappeared right round the corner of one of those sheds, and then she went to buy a hat.

It was a pretty, stitched cotton hat with a white-lined brim to match her collar. She also bought a cork toupee, to wear about the place out at Yattabilla, as the storeman assured her that that was what many of the country women favoured, because it was light and cool, as well as practical and sun-stopping. She got a small one for Skeet, too, in the boys' department, and a pair of sandals, because she had noticed that that was what the other children in the bus had worn, and she knew Skeet would want to be the same. In his ankle-socks and lacing shoes, he had looked odd, because the others had not even socks – just bare brown legs.

Kids like to be the same as other kids, Madeleine. Steve's words echoed in her mind as the man was wrapping the sandals in a piece of brown paper for her. Drat Steve! She wished she could forget all those nasty things he had said. They were all the more nasty because, largely, they happened to be true!

After Maddie had finished in the clothing store, she bought her driving manual, and then crossed over the street to the garage to get the battery. She was quite horrified at the price! Her own purse would not run to such expense, and Maddie spent a short while wrestling with her conscience. Could she mark it down on the Yattabilla account? Steve had said she must do that, for necessities. And you could say that that battery was a necessity, couldn't you? Without it the Buick would not go, and unless the Buick went, Maddie would be unable to teach herself how to drive it.

By the time Steve got those accounts and studied the individual items on them, she would have achieved her purpose.

'Just mark it down to Yattabilla,' she told the garageman calmly.

Maddie's next discovery was that batteries are not only extremely expensive, they are heavy, as well. Too heavy, that is, to carry about Noonday with one, until the school bus left.

Maddie was dithering as to whether she should persuade the garage man to deliver it to the bus, or persuade the bus driver to call for it at the garage, when a cheerful voice hailed her.

'Maddie? It is!'

Tom Simson shook her gloved hand enthusiastically.

'By Jove, it's good to see you! I wondered for a minute if I was dreaming. What are you doing in Noonday – I mean, *here*, of all places?' He cast an eye at their oil-stained surroundings.

'Well, as a matter of fact, I've bought a battery, and I don't quite know what I'm going to do with it next.' Maddie went on to explain just *why* she needed that battery.

Tom seemed highly amused at the whole adventure.

'And do you know what to do with it *after* you get it home?' he asked dubiously. 'No? You hope Lal might?'

He stood a moment after Maddie had spoken, wrapped in thought, and then he smiled at her disarmingly.

'Look, Maddie, I've a much better idea. You're not going out on that bus this afternoon. I'll run you and Skeet home instead, and tune up that car for you.'

'But, Tom, it's sixty miles!'

Tom roared with laughter.

'Sixty miles, she says! Oh, Maddie, that's an English remark, if ever there was one! These aren't your narrow little hedge-bound lanes, remember, it's the wide open spaces. Sixty's nothing to Australians, especially country Australians. Goodness, girl, we'll go a hundred miles to a dance and back, and think nothing of it. No, I insist,' as she started to protest again. 'It'll be my pleasure, and anyway, I rather fancy myself as a mechanic!'

'Tom, really – I don't know how to thank you.' How kind, how warmhearted these country people were! And he wasn't only going to drive them home, he was going to get that car going for her as well!

'You can thank me by having lunch with me,' said Tom firmly. 'One o'clock at the Royal – that's it down there, the place with the green awning. It'll only be steak and eggs, but it's good steak. Will you?'

Maddie smiled warmly.

'I'd love that, Tom. I'll be there at one o'clock — and thank you again.'

'On the contrary, thank *you*, lady,' corrected Tom with mock gallantry, before he, too, went off in the direction of the sale-yards.

Maddie wandered around the town for a time. The day was getting hotter as it wore on, and after her early start and the long trek to the twin-fork, she soon got tired of walking about, and after she had ordered a cool lemon drink in an Italian café, with a huge fan whirring softly above her head, she sat for a while enjoying a respite from the sun outside. Everyone seemed nice in this town! Many of the people had smiled when she passed them in the street, and some even went so far as to nod and say 'G'day.'

Maddie had known all along that Noonday was that sort of place. You could tell by the look of it, in some indefinable way. Here, in Noonday, people seemed to have time to think of other people. They were considerate and interested, without being actually inquisitive.

The café proprietor came over and leaned his forearms on the formica table at which she was sitting.

'The drink's O.K.?'

'It's delicious, thank you.'

'It's fresh lemon, see.' He jerked his head towards the back of the premises. 'Off the lemon tree. We gotta lemon tree out there, and always she has lemons! On a hot day, very good, eh?'

'It's really lovely. Thank you.' Maddie smiled her wide, warm, spontaneous smile — the one Skeet adored — and the Italian smiled, too.

'You come the nex' time,' he said to Maddie when she got up to leave, 'And you get more lemon, eh? Always we have the lemons — the best in Noonday!'

'Till next time,' promised Maddie in farewell.

'Sure, till the nex' time.' The Italian showed his beautiful white teeth in a big, broad smile. He seemed very pleased.

Out in the street·once more, Maddie hesitated a moment, and then she, too, turned in the direction of those tin-roofed sheds. She could hear, even at a distance, the continuous bleating of large numbers of sheep, and there seemed to be occasional shouting and a constant cloud of dust. Behind the sheds, Maddie found that all the sale activity was taking place in the open air. The yards consisted of a series of pens, strongly fenced, and on those fences sat a lot of men. Some were buyers, but a lot were simply looking on. When the auctioneer had sold the sheep in one pen, the men all got down off that fence and moved on to sit on the next one. Maddie thought she had never seen such a funny sight – rows and rows of men, all straddling the fences, all with those wide felt hats pulled down to hide their expressionless brown faces so that you couldn't see their eyes at all. She wondered, indeed, if they themselves could see what the auctioneer was doing – or did they just listen to his voice?

She watched with interest, amazed at the speed of the auctioneer's patter. All sorts of unfamiliar terms rang in her ears – wethers, hoggets, two-tooths, broken mouths, sound mouths, cast for age, off-shears. To her it was an incomprehensible dialect, and she marvelled that those rows of brown-chinned, broad-hatted, apparently eyeless men must know what it was all about.

Steve must have been one of the faceless figures sitting on the fence. Suddenly he was there beside her.

'That's a pretty smart hat! I'm glad you got one.'

'Thank you,' she returned politely. 'I'm pleased you like it.'

She felt, quite suddenly, a little bit breathless, a little bit unsteady. Steve always seemed to have this effect on her, she realized irritably. She wished he didn't make her feel so young – so – so unsure. Standing there beside him, she felt dwarfed. There was no doubt he was a handsome creature, arrogant even when his lean brown face was caked with dust and sweat as it was at this minute. His deep, mahogany-coloured tan only served to make his steady grey eyes a lighter colour than they really were, with an attraction all their own. It didn't take away any of that keenness that made her feel so uncomfortable, though. It was the same with his teeth. They appeared white and strong and made a pleasant contrast to the brownness, but they could snap shut with disapproval, too, just when you were hoping they wouldn't!

Right now, his lips were curling in a rather irresistible way.

'You'd better come out of the sun, Madeleine.' He drew her into a small patch of shade near one of the sheds. 'Watch from here, it will be cooler and less dusty. In a little while I'll take you for some lunch.'

Maddie was taken aback.

'Oh! Well – er – actually I have already made arrangements to have lunch with someone else – with – with Tom, I mean. At the – the Royal, at one o'clock.' Her cheeks were afire, and the words seemed to tumble out. How she wished she could control that angry blush!

Steve was watching her all the time she was speaking. His expression did not appreciably change, but his eyes got the least bit more narrow, if anything, and they held that depth of intentness that made her feel so awkward. His strong brown fingers caressed his chin in a steady, imperturbable sort of way.

'I – see,' he finally said, and Maddie didn't much like the way he said *that*, either! 'You certainly don't let the grass grow under your feet, little one!'

'I – don't understand,' mumbled Maddie.

'No? Ah, well, perhaps not.' He straightened, glanced down at his sweat-damp shirt and dusty boots. 'In any case, I dare say young Simson's in a more fit state to take a lady out to lunch than I am!' He looked at his watch. 'I'll take you home when school comes out, Madeleine. We can collect Skeet on the way.'

She was now really scarlet with embarrassment.

'Well, as a matter of fact, I – I mean, Tom said he'd take

us home, too, thank you. I – I mean, he offered. He – he *wants* to.'

'I'm sure he does,' drawled Steve, adding in a murmur, 'Youth will to youth, and it was ever thus!'

'P-pardon?'

'Nothing, Madeleine. A misquotation, merely, but appropriate in the circumstances. Off you go then, and enjoy yourself.'

'Thank you, Steve. And – er – thank you for telling me about the hat.'

Steve's grin was sardonic.

'Noble of me, wasn't it? Just think, if you had died of sunstroke, Yattabilla would be mine!'

Before Maddie could reply, he was gone – just a faceless figure in a slanting felt hat, amongst all the other faceless figures sitting on the fence.

CHAPTER SEVEN

MADDIE enjoyed her lunch with Tom, up to a point. But only up to a point.

She could not say exactly where her reservations lay, because, as Tom had promised, the steak was good, and so were the two fried eggs that went along with it. His company was amusing, too, and she felt relaxed with him, so that was not the reason for this feeling of incompleteness, of anticlimax, either.

Maddie looked across to where Tom sat, and saw his round young face change under her dreamy gaze. Suddenly the roundness had gone. It was replaced by leaner, tougher cheeks, with deep grooves beside the mouth. And the eyes weren't Tom's merry blue ones any more. They had become grey and grave and watchful, and they seemed to be piercing right into her mind, trying to tell her something. Yes, they were Steve Darley's eyes, and they were trying to tell her just why she was not enjoying this luncheon with Tom as much as she had thought she would.

Maddie blinked, and was relieved to see Steve's image fade. It was replaced by Tom's once more. She realized that she had almost dozed off, between the heat and a meal that was larger than she was accustomed to eating in the middle of the day.

What nasty tricks one's mind could play at times. How silly! As if she could possibly *prefer* that it should be Steve sitting there opposite! Her mind ought to know better than that. It ought to know that she loathed the very sight of Steve, and all that he represented. The man was a positive threat to her inheritance! That's what he was! Maybe that was why she couldn't stop thinking about him, and why his image had even come between herself and Tom, sitting here in the Royal having lunch.

'Ice-cream, Maddie?'

'Mm, yes, thank you.'

'And some fruit salad along with it,' her companion said to the waitress. 'And a pot of tea.' He turned back to Maddie. 'We all drink tea out here, so I didn't bother to consult. O.K.? Tea and beer – the national beverages, you might say.'

'Yes, I've noticed that.' Maddie smiled, remembering the gay young crowd of Australians on the boat coming out. They had consumed vast quantities of beer, some brashly and noisily, others quietly and steadily, but they had seemed to want beer with everything they did, whether it was swimming and deck sports, or dancing and housey-housey. The national beverage? Yes, Tom could be right.

'Cigarette?' When Maddie declined, Tom lit one for himself, and leaned back. 'Tell me, Maddie – and shut me up for an interfering fool if you like! – but wouldn't it be nicer for you to live in town during the week, when Skeet's at school, and just go out to Yattabilla at week-ends? From what I've heard, the house isn't – well, up to much, is it? No offence to your dad, mind you, Maddie, but one gets to hear things out in the bush, you know. Yarns sort of get around, and I can't help feeling, from what I've heard, that you would be a good deal more comfortable in town. I could maybe even fix you up with a job, if you'd like that? My old man knows just about everybody hereabouts, and it wouldn't be hard to find you something to keep you amused.'

How often had not her own mind run along just these lines! Here was Tom suggesting the very thing she had yearned for, and Maddie could not accept. She bit her lip in vexation.

There was nothing for it but to tell Tom about that binding legal clause in her father's will – about that 'term of residence' which was already proving almost more than Maddie could cope with, now that she had to do it alone, without Skeet.

Maddie told Tom about the will, but only the bit that

applied to herself. She could not say why, but some inner sense of caution and pride prevented her from even mentioning Steve's name in this connection.

'So you see, Tom, I'll have to stay there to comply with the terms. Of course I'd much rather be in Noonday, but there's no help for it. And anyway –' she brightened – 'if I can only get that car going, and learn to drive it, I won't feel nearly so lonely and cut off. You *do* see how important it is for me, Tom? How much it means to me?'

'Yes, I certainly do, Maddie!' Tom gave her a warm look of undisguised admiration. 'You leave that bit to me, eh? I'll get her going for you, like a bird, I promise. I'll tune her up, and give you a few preliminary hints, and then I'll keep an eye on your progress whenever I get the chance. How's that?'

'Marvellous! Oh, Tom, thank you! You don't know what it means to have someone on my side.'

He looked puzzled.

'On your side, Maddie? Lord, you must be out of your mind, my girl! I can't think of any chap who *wouldn't* want to be on your side, sweetie. My motives are purely selfish, I warn you! I'm merely trying to beat the others to it, to be on your side first.' He winked at her, checked the time. 'I'll have to go. Lunch-break is over, I'm afraid.'

Tom stood up, reached his hat from the hook above his head, and guided her out towards the street. Outside, he nodded to two aboriginal stockmen as they passed. When they said, 'G'day, Tom,' he replied, ' 'Day, Jackie, Billy.'

'Who are they?' asked Maddie, eyeing the retreating figures with interest. They wore open shirts – the striped variety that should have an accompanying collar attached to the neck but hadn't – khaki trousers and heeled boots, and on their heads they sported quite the most dilapidated felt hats that Maddie had ever seen. The older one had a tangled beard of a surprising and unexpected grey, wrinkled black skin, and ageless brown eyes.

'They're two of Steve Darley's stockmen,' Tom informed

her. 'The older one's called Billy Sundown, a bit of a local character. He's supposed to be a descendant of King Billy himself. I'm surprised you haven't seen him around the place out there. I believe Yattabilla was pretty much under-manned when your father died, Maddie, and now the Bibbi men work the two properties together, more or less, for the time being. Decent of Darley, but he's that sort of chap — and anyway, he's a trustee or something, isn't he?'

Or *something*! Maddie swallowed, trying in vain to ignore the sinister portent of Tom's innocent observations. So that was what Steve was up to! He was so sure that he was going to get Yattabilla, that already he was working it along with his own place. He couldn't even wait a year.

He must feel very certain indeed. He must be very sure that Maddie would not manage to 'stick things out'. Well, she'd show him! His underhand connivings would only serve to strengthen her personal resolution to defeat his ends. She would stay at Yattabilla, no matter how awful it was, and when the year was up, it would be hers. Hers and Skeet's, that is. And in the meantime, if she could only learn to drive that car so that she was able to get about a bit, that too would help to make life a little more bearable.

Decent, indeed! It was all Maddie could do to refrain from an indignant snort. If only Tom knew! Still, he was better not to know that Steve was involved in any way, for such was Steve Darley's charm and influence that Maddie would not put it past him to go to work on Tom, and win him around to his way of thinking. Maddie didn't want that to happen. She wanted Tom to be on *her* side, and most of all, she wanted him to help her to learn how to drive that car. If Steve found out about that, he would doubtless put a stop to it, as he would to anything that was going to make her life at Yattabilla more pleasant, so it was necessary to keep absolutely quiet just now. Tom could think Steve was decent, if he liked — but she, Maddie, knew better!

'I'll see you later, then, Maddie.' Tom was speaking to her. 'You meet Skeet when he comes out of school, and see that he doesn't get on the bus. Then you can both come around to the office, and we'll collect the battery at the garage on the way out of town. Right?'

'Right, Tom.' She smiled her gratitude.

'Down that side-street, then. You'll see the name, with "Stock & Station Agents" painted on the windows. You can't miss it. See you.'

'See you, Tom.'

When he had left her, Maddie wandered over to the park. There were pretty trees and flower-beds there, and a narrow path along the river-bank, where walking was cool and pleasant. Further on, there was a shallow, walled paddling-pool, with a fountain in the middle.

She sat on a nearby seat, watching several tiny tots splashing water over each other while their mothers looked on patiently, and when it was the time for Skeet to come out of school, she got up and walked, more quickly now, in that direction.

Her heart was beating faster in the anticipation of seeing Skeet. How she had missed him, all this week! Maddie's pulse slowed again to a monotonous tattoo as she remembered all the other, similar weeks that were to come. There were a whole fifty-two of them in a year, weren't there? The only cheering thought was that some of the fifty-two would be school holidays, when she and Skeet could be together all the time.

. He came out of school cockily, one of a number of small jostling figures, who called high-pitched farewells to the teacher at the steps, as they came rushing forth.

When he got near, Maddie saw that he had abandoned his ankle-socks. Beneath his grubby knees his legs were bare, like the other children's – a sign that Skeet himself had already recognized the need to be like the others, and had taken what personal steps he could to achieve this end. She was glad that she had bought those sandals. He could wear them to school on Monday, like all the rest.

Maddie felt that she was seeing Skeet in a new light.

They had never been apart before, and now, for the first time, she was able to take an objective look at her little brother. She could swear that he had actually grown during the past week! His spiky red hair was as unruly as ever, his freckles as profuse, but he seemed taller than she had thought – more self-reliant, too. He was spindly, and maybe frailer-looking than these sturdy country-reared children. Of course, his skin wasn't the sort to take a tan, and it was the thinness of his limbs that had always worried her. Now Maddie was aware, for perhaps the first time ever, of an underlying toughness in Skeet's wiry frame. With surprise she realized that, far from needing her constant care and protection, her young brother was well able to take care of himself!

It appeared that already he was fitting happily into his new environment. There was a certain amount of good-natured scuffling and repartee with his mates before he even bothered to acknowledge her presence, and when he did, it was with a rather unenthusiastic, ' 'Lo, Maddie. Can't I stay a while longer? The bus doesn't go for ages yet.'

'We aren't going on the bus, Skeet. Tom Simson's driving us home. If you come now, you can have an ice-cream before we leave.'

Skeet hesitated, but his playmate's exclamation of 'Lucky coot!' was enough to send him off with Maddie without further argument, and he paused only to turn and make a hideous face at his small friend, who giggled as he walked away.

He regaled them with his week's adventures the whole way out to Yattabilla, stopping only to hop out and in when the gates came along. This time he had no hesitation in opening all the different catches. 'He's not too young to learn, Madeleine.' Maddie remembered Steve's reproving words. They had seemed tough and unfeeling at the time, but she was forced – very grudgingly – to admit that he had been right.

When they arrived at the homestead, Skeet leapt out of

the car and ran to see Etta, his hen, in order to reassure himself that Maddie had indeed been attending to her faithfully, as she had sworn she would. Satisfied on that score, he reappeared to find Tom drinking a beer, and his sister making tea.

Afterwards, he followed Tom out to the garage and watched with interest as he began to overhaul the car. Skeet had always been possessed of an innate curiosity about the workings of engines, and it was pleasant to sit on a drum, feeling satisfyingly full of tea and cakes, watching Tom's greasy fingers following terminal leads, checking points and plugs. When the overhaul got to a certain stage, Tom reversed the car right out of the garage, and took Skeet for a run down the track.

When they came back, he lifted the bonnet, made a few more minor adjustments, and then sent Skeet in to get his sister.

For nearly two hours Tom put Maddie through her paces. He was a patient instructor, first explaining the basic movements of the gears, the action of the clutch and accelerator. After that, he made his pupil go through all the motions herself, and finally he started the engine, and, with Maddie at the wheel, they began to make hesitant progress over the tracks about the homestead.

It was dark by the time Tom said he must be going, and a perspiring but triumphant Maddie slid thankfully from the driving-seat and allowed her tutor to put the Buick away in the garage.

'Not bad. Not bad at all!' That was Tom.

'I'll practise like anything, Tom. I'll do it every day.'

'Keep trying as much as I've shown you, Maddie, and we'll do it again next week. How about coming in again on Friday, like you did today, and I'll take you back.'

Maddie hesitated, sorely tempted. There would probably be a lorry passing the twin-fork again, or at least some sort of vehicle was bound to pass if she got there early. It was only a matter of waiting, and then hitching a lift. The thing that made her hesitate was her promise to Steve. Why a promise made to someone who was himself so unscrupulous should be so binding to her, Maddie could not really have said. Perhaps, if she were honest with herself, she would admit that she was just the least bit frightened of Steve. The thought of being caught by him, standing at the twin-fork waiting for a lift, when he had expressly asked her not to do it again, was enough to make her go weak about the knees and shake her head, more adamantly, at Tom.

'I couldn't, Tom. There's no means of getting in, short of chancing a lift, and I – I didn't much enjoy doing that this morning. I felt – er – sort of nervous.'

'Quite right, too,' he approved. 'I don't think you'd better do that again, either. Tell you what, Maddie, I'll come and collect you.'

'Tom, you can't.'

'Can't I? You watch me! It'll be early, but you won't mind that, will you? So long as I'm ready when the office opens, my time's my own, Maddie, and I can't think of a more pleasant way of spending it, so positively no ifs or buts.'

'I don't know what to say. It's much too kind. But maybe, after another lot of lessons, I'll be able to practise enough to get a licence quite soon,' she added hopefully.

'Sure you will. You're a natural!' he grinned. 'Well, see you on Friday. Be ready.'

'I'll be ready on Friday, Tom,' Maddie called, waving to the retreating car, while Skeet yelled 'Goodbye' from his position on the top wire of the fence. With an answering toot-a-toot, Tom was off, and Maddie and Skeet stepped carefully over the weak places on the verandah, and went inside out of the darkness.

Maddie felt tired, but cheerful. She had actually managed to drive that car, and it was simpler than she had imagined. Admittedly it had leapt around like a startled kangaroo at first, but by the time she had stopped, she had been beginning to get the feel of the wheel beneath her hands and the pedals under her feet. She was sure she could do it! It was only a matter of practice!

Maddie indulged Skeet hopelessly during the week-end, making all his favourite dishes, and some treacle toffee into the bargain. Suddenly life seemed worthwhile again, because he was back with her. Skeet was her reason for living, she had discovered – or at any rate, her reason for living at Yattabilla. His piquant little face hovering over the dinner made the cooking of it a pleasure, and the sight of his skinny form squatting patiently beside Henrietta down in the fowl-yard gave Maddie herself a feeling of peace and stability.

When the time came to say goodbye to him again on Monday morning, Maddie found that she had not quite the same sense of deprivation that she had experienced the previous week. It was impossible to feel sorry for Skeet, strutting proudly over to the bus in his new brown sandals, looking extremely pleased with himself. Rather did she feel sorry for herself! But that would not do, either, Maddie told herself determinedly, when the bus had rumbled out of sight. She must keep busy, and that way she would manage somehow to stave off the loneliness that threatened.

At least there was something to be busy *at*, she reminded herself, and that something was the car!

Maddie drove it at every opportunity throughout the week, uncertainly at first, and then with increasing confidence. She did not attempt to make turns, because Tom had not shown her how to do that yet, but she practised the gear-changes and stopping and starting, and in the evenings she studied her manual, so that she would get to know her signals and traffic code. The thought of traffic caused Maddie to smile wryly. At Yattabilla there was not even a slope on which to try hill starts, let alone another car to contend with, but she would have to learn about those things, to prepare for the time when she could drive into Noonday to get her licence. Tom had said that he would help her to get a permit, and that he would accompany her into town when the great day came.

She was ready when Tom arrived to collect her on Friday morning. She had put on the same cotton two-piece as she had worn on the previous visit, because it was the only suitable garment she possessed. This time, however, she did not need her canvas shoes, because there was to be no long walk to the twin-fork. Instead, she was able to step straight into Tom's comfortable car.

It was pleasantly cool travelling over the plain at that early hour, but, as before, the day's heat was beginning to make itself felt by the time they reached Noonday.

Tom surprised Maddie by taking her straight to his own house – 'to wash off the dust,' he explained with a grin. After she had done that, his mother took her out on to a trellised verandah and insisted on giving her what amounted to a second breakfast, of grapefruit, toast, and deliciously refreshing China tea with lemon. Mrs. Simson was kind and welcoming and uncritical, as the Noonday people all seemed to be. Maddie chatted to her happily, making her laugh at some of the innocent pickles into which she had got herself as a newcomer to Yattabilla.

Maddie managed to make it all sound fun – a big, humorous adventure.

She did not mention the loneliness, or the spiders when she had arrived, or the mouse-holes in the mattresses, or the dead blowflies, or even the snake. They were things that she did not want to remember, so she talked instead about the deafening noise the frogs made in the creek – how they had kept her awake at first, but now amounted to a sort of lullaby – about Etta, the hen, and Skeet's attempts at fishing, and her own at driving.

When Tom left to open the Agency office, he said that he would see Maddie again after school. This time he would not be able to have lunch with her, as his father was away valuing a property, and he was holding the fort, but Mrs. Simson would love to have her for lunch anyway.

Maddie protested at such intrusions upon their hospitality, but they were jointly insistent.

'It's no trouble, my dear,' Mrs. Simson assured her warmly, 'and it will do me good to have some young company about the house. I've a daughter, too, you know – did Tom tell you about his sister? She's about your own age, Maddie, nursing in Sydney. How I miss my Jill, but it's something she always wanted to do ever since she was a little girl, and one mustn't stand in their way. I suppose I'm lucky that Tom, at least, has decided to follow in his father's footsteps, and won't ever be too far away, for that reason. When he decides to get married, he'll have to have a house of his own, of course, but he'll be in Noonday to be near the office.'

Maddie helped her hostess to carry the breakfast dishes in from the verandah and to wash them up. The house was modern, small, air-conditioned and delightfully cool. There were terrazzo floors in the kitchen and bathroom, and tiles on the verandah which completely encircled the house – a bit different from the rotting planks at Yattabilla, thought Maddie wryly.

She enjoyed helping with the small amount of housework, and when she had done all she could, Mrs. Simson made another pot of tea, gave her some magazines, and told her to amuse herself on the verandah for a while.

'You were up so early, dear, and I'm sure you could do with a rest. You must work quite hard out there at Yattabilla, Maddie, even if you do have some fun, too. It's common knowledge that Gerald didn't do a thing to that homestead for years. He rather lost heart once your – once he was on his own.'

Once your mother had run out on him? Was *that* what Mrs. Simson had been going to say? That was what Steve had said, anyway. That was how *he* had put it.

'Oh, it's not too bad, really,' Maddie heard herself defending the old place loyally. 'The kerosene fridge works all right, once you get to know its little foibles, and most of the time there's electricity. And when the plant runs down, and Lal is away, we have the Tilleys.'

'Oh, my dear!' Tom's mother looked so genuinely distressed that Maddie wondered if she had been tactless in mentioning it.

After lunch, Mrs. Simson suggested that they walk around to the shopping centre together.

'I've just a very few things to order, Maddie, and you'll be able to go on to the school to collect your brother from there. That suit you?'

'Perfectly, thank you. And thank you, too, for the delicious lunch, and all your kindness. I've had a beautifully lazy day.'

'And deserved it, too, dear, I'm sure. Why, hallo, Steve!'

Steve Darley's fingers lifted the gate latch neatly back into place behind him. He raised his broad-brimmed hat respectfully to the older woman.

'Good afternoon, Doreen,' he said to Mrs. Simson, then, looking past her to where Maddie had adopted a frozen stance, he added more coolly, 'And to you, too, Madeleine.'

'Do come in, Steve, won't you, and have a drink? Beer? A whisky?' Tom's mother suggested coaxingly. She seemed pleased and surprised to see Steve coming up her path, and made her delight at his visit quite obvious.

Maddie wished that she could share Mrs. Simson's pleasure at the sight of him, but she couldn't. Neither must she give way to the nasty sinking feeling that had suddenly assailed her stomach.

The sinking sensation eased a little bit as she heard Steve decline the invitation.

'Not just now, thanks all the same,' he replied politely, standing in front of Mrs. Simson and smiling down at her. 'I just came in to say that I'll be taking Madeleine and Skeet home from school when the children come out. I happened to have to come to town today in any case. I'm meeting Kareena off the plane.'

'Oh, I see. Did you want me to tell Tom, Steve?'

'No need. I've already seen him,' returned Steve coolly, still talking to the older woman, and completely ignoring Maddie. They both were, in fact! Steve seemed to have that effect on people. He could possess their entire attention to the exclusion of everybody else, and that was what he was doing now with Mrs. Simson. She appeared pleased and flattered that he had come to see her at all, and the fact that he had high-handedly altered her son's and Maddie's plans without consulting either of them did not seem to be causing Mrs. Simson the same degree of pique as it did Maddie.

'I know Geoff's away on a valuation, so it will save Tom the run out later on,' Steve was saying. 'I called in at Yattabilla on my way in, and Mrs. Lawrence said he'd taken Madeleine into town very early. I've told Tom I'll handle the return trip myself.'

But what about my driving lessons? Maddie wanted to wail – only she stopped herself, because Steve must not know about those. They were her secret – hers and Tom's.

Oh, dear! Why had Steve to come into Noonday today of all days? She had thought it an opportune time because there was no sale today and few country men in town. Of course she had not known anything about him coming in to meet somebody whose name was Kareena. Now her visit to town seemed to have lost its purpose, except for her meeting with Mrs. Simson, that is. She had to admit that, up until the moment Steve had appeared, her day had been enjoyable, and it was warming to think that she had made a real friend in Noonday. She could understand, too, that Tom had not wanted to make an issue of the drive back to Yattabilla. There were plenty of other days ahead, and on their slender acquaintance, it would have appeared odd if he had protested too much when Steve offered to take her home, especially as Steve almost passed her homestead on his way to Bibbi.

Maddie knew that she could count on Tom not to have

mentioned the driving lessons, and Skeet, too, had been sworn to silence, because, as she impressed upon him, it would be such fun to suddenly surprise everybody with the fact that she could drive. Skeet had giggled, and agreed to say nothing to anyone.

When she and Mrs. Simson were walking together at the shopping centre some time later, Maddie heard a deep droning noise up in the sky, and looking up, she saw a neat silver plane circle once at the edge of the trees, and then gently descend until it was out of sight behind the houses. That must be the plane that Steve had come to meet, she supposed. It would be the plane with Kareena in it.

Maddie had been wondering about that, but up to this moment she had not liked to mention it for fear of being thought inquisitive. Now she asked as casually as she could,

'Who is Kareena, Mrs. Simson? I suppose that will be her plane? I hadn't realized there was a plane service to Noonday.'

'There isn't, dear,' replied Tom's mother dryly. 'Kareena always charters a plane especially to bring her. That's the way Kareena works, you see. If things don't suit her, she finds a way around them, or else she alters them until they do. She doesn't like trains, and she does like planes, so she simply hires one whenever she wants to go any great distance from Sydney. It's as simple as that – to Kareena.'

'But who *is* she?'

'Kareena? She's the niece of a very prominent grazier who had a string of properties starting on the west side of Noonday and continuing almost to the centre of Australia itself. Her uncle's dead now, but he and Steve Darley's father were great friends – natural, I suppose, as the Darleys are in a big way out here too. Kareena still comes up for all the big events, and often stays at Bibbi for them.' Mrs. Simson adjusted the string bag she carried to a more comfortable position on her arm, declining Maddie's offer to take it from her with a smile. 'No, it's not heavy, Maddie, it just kept catching on the clasp of my handbag. That's better.' She returned to her previous topic. 'It's early for Kareena to be paying a visit, I must say. The next big thing on the social calendar is the Polo Carnival, and that's not till autumn. It isn't like her to come right in the middle of the summer heat! But of course –' Mrs. Simson looked momentarily coy – 'there may be more to it than meets the eye. I mean, obviously Steve has *asked* her, hasn't he, when it's out of season that she has come. We've all been wondering for some time now about those two. After all, he is a very attractive man, you know.'

That was something Maddie *didn't* know! Attractive? Well, yes, in a way, she supposed he was. In a physical way, that is – if you cared for the tough, authoritative, insensitive type – which Maddie didn't. Unscrupulous, overbearing, domineering, autocratic – there was no end to the list of undesirable adjectives she could apply to Steve Darley, but of course she didn't say them out loud. It was more tactful to pass off Mrs. Simson's glowing statement with a noncommittal murmur, the sort that could be taken for agreement.

When they had finished their shopping, they went into the Italian café which Maddie had discovered on her previous visit. Mrs. Simson seemed to know about the lemon tree, because she ordered two fresh lemon drinks with ice, and said to Maddie, 'The most cooling drinks in town, these are. There's something about *fresh* lemons that a bottle can't capture, don't you think? Mm! Isn't that fan nice on one's face!'

She lifted her head to catch the breeze from the big circular fan above them, and Maddie did the same.

It was very hot indeed today – a dry, intense, still heat that made one's clothes stick to one's body. Maddie knew that her little cotton two-piece, which had started the day so crisp and smart, was now as limp as a rag. Thank goodness she did not have to go home in the old school bus. That was at least something for which to be thankful, if Tom was not now taking her, and there was no doubt that Steve's big Chev was fast and smooth and comfortable.

When she had thanked Tom's mother once again, and had said goodbye, Maddie made her way slowly up to the school-house. By the time she got there she was perspiring freely again, and her white shoes were covered with dust. Her cotton gloves were grimy, too. Ah, well! Maddie drew them off resignedly and tucked them in her bag. They seemed to soil more readily than her nylon ones, and it was better to wear none than to have dirty ones. Maddie had always been fastidious about nice clean gloves.

The children had hardly run out of school, scuffling and pushing each other like the last time, than Steve's big car approached.

As it took a wide turn outside the building and drew up to face the direction from whence it had come, Maddie could see that Steve already had a passenger. Sitting beside him in the front passenger seat was an elegant figure in dark sun-glasses and a sleeveless dress of hyacinth blue linen.

This must be Kareena.

Skeet pitched his school-bag unceremoniously into the back seat and scrambled in after it, and Steve, who had come around to open the door for Maddie, hauled him back with an equal lack of ceremony.

'Ladies first,' he rebuked sternly, then nodded to Maddie to get in, while he kept a restraining grasp on her bother's shoulder.

His nearness and sternness made her dithery. She slid past him into the seat, and muttered a greeting to her fellow passenger, and Kareena turned sideways to give a cool and markedly unenthusiastic reply.

It was only then that Maddie realized just who was hiding behind those dark glasses. She did not really need to see that perfect profile and feminine neck. She didn't need to see the beautiful, dark upswept hair, or the lovely slender hand that rested its manicured fingers on Steve's steering-wheel. The voice alone would have been enough. For Maddie there was no mistaking the clear, resonant, pure diction of the goddess herself!

CHAPTER EIGHT

'KAREENA, this is Madeleine Masterton, and her brother Skeet. Kareena Powell, Madeleine.'

The goddess removed her sunglasses for an instant, and regarded Maddie with a curious, pale blue stare.

'Haven't we met before somewhere? No, it's obviously not possible.' With an elegant shrug of her slender shoulders, and a rather distasteful glance at Skeet, Kareena answered her own question. 'Please don't put your *extremely* dirty sandals near my hat-box, will you, little boy?'

Her voice was husky, and carried the sort of sarcastic adult humour that was completely lost on Skeet.

He mumbled 'Sorry!' got so red that his freckles disappeared altogether, and he hastily tucked his feet in at a safer distance from the cream hide case beside them. Maddie felt overwhelmed with pity for her little brother's embarrassment, and indignation on his behalf.

Surprisingly, it was Steve himself who came to the rescue.

Maddie saw him watching Skeet in the driving mirror, and then he asked, 'How's school, Skeet, old chap? I hear your football's coming on fast. You'll never guess who told me that!'

'Who, Steve?' Skeet leaned forward eagerly, his misery receding.

'Peters himself. He's the one who picks the team, isn't he?'

'Yes, that's right. Gee, Steve, did Peters *really* tell you I was getting good?'

'Certainly he did. I wouldn't be saying it right now if he hadn't.'

'How do you know Peters, Steve?'

'I know his dad, that's how.'

'He's got a sister, too. D'you know her? Her name's Susan, and she's really the soppiest kid!' Skeet's voice was loud with disgust. 'I think girls are *all* soppy, Steve – or most of 'em. Gosh, in school they cry for just about anything. They spend their whole time crying about something, even if it isn't anything much, don't you think, Steve?'

Steve's eyes in the driving mirror met Maddie's for an instant.

'I guess they grow up, Skeet,' was his tolerant reply. 'They all grow up, and then they'd rather die than be seen crying. Haven't you noticed that yourself, Skeet? You will, when you grow up too.'

Steve's mouth was smiling, but his eyes weren't. Maddie could see that they were quite serious before he turned them back to the road ahead.

'I suppose so,' returned Skeet more thoughtfully. 'Maddie's grown up, and *she* never cries.'

'Exactly,' Steve said succinctly.

Kareena moved impatiently against the leather upholstery at her back. She seemed amused.

'Dear me, Steve darling, I'd no idea you could be so chatty with children. I'm seeing you in a new light, pet! So patient and sweet – quite avuncular, in fact.'

'Maybe you don't know me quite as well as you thought, Kareena.' Steve's reply carried a dangerous smoothness. 'I've always liked kids.'

If Maddie had been the other girl, she would have taken the note in Steve's voice as a warning to change the subject, but Kareena didn't seem to feel that way. Perhaps it was because she had known Steve for such a long time that she felt she could now rush in where Maddie would have feared to tread.

'Quite, darling. So long as they don't make themselves heard *too* much, I adore them, too. As for not knowing you, that bit fascinates me! I thought I knew you very well – very well indeed, in fact – but I like discovering new facets in people, don't you? I'd hate a man who withheld nothing of his character from me! I like a little mystery in my friendships. It makes them more challenging, and more *promising*, I think.'

'You always were a girl for a challenge, weren't you, Kareena?' Steve chuckled indulgently.

'Well, you know what I mean, darling. I don't care for obvious people. I lose patience with these naïve young things who fawn all over one – it becomes so boring. Of course it's fun at Madeleine's age—' Kareena turned her head again, to address Maddie herself – 'That nice young Simson boy, for instance. I hear he's quite smitten with you. I'd encourage him if I were you, my dear. They're a good sound family, and he's wholesome, if a bit ingenuous. I'd say you'd be quite well matched – even lucky to get him.'

'How kind you are to be interested in my welfare,' replied Maddie meekly, although she was burning up with fury at the other's hateful condescension. Her eyes were angry, but she had managed to make her voice submissive and honeyed, and was rewarded at the sight of Steve's lips twitching with a quickly suppressed smile.

'I think Madeleine would prefer to look after her own welfare, Kareena, without us offering her any advice, however helpful,' he interposed calmly. 'Tell me, how are the Harris family doing, since they moved to Melbourne? Do you hear?'

He had adroitly steered his companion on to a new course.

Kareena talked animatedly of mutual acquaintances in the major cities. It appeared that she and Steve shared a wide circle of friends, many of high social standing, by the sound of her conversation. Maddie and Skeet were effectively excluded, but Maddie could only feel relief at that. She knew that in Kareena's particular sort of barbed repartee, she would be hopelessly bested, so she was glad just to lie back in her corner as the miles skimmed past, only half listening.

Skeet had been lulled to sleep by the constant buzz of voices from the front seat, concerned only with topics that bored him. His head had fallen sideways and his mouth was slightly open. When the first gate came, he was still asleep, and Maddie acted fast, scrambling out in his stead.

She noticed that, this time, Steve didn't prevent her and insist on the front passenger doing it, as he had that other time! Maddie couldn't resist a smile at the thought of Kareena's face if he had done that! She lifted the latch, glad that she had already had some personal practice at gate-opening with both Ted Widmore and Tom. At least she wasn't making a fool of herself in front of the goddess, she thought acidly, as she flicked the gate back into position and returned to the car.

Steve made no comment at the time, but after the last gate had been opened and shut, he said 'Thank you, Madeleine' when she got back into the car. Kareena, of course, said nothing at all, but then Maddie had not expected her to.

At Yattabilla Steve helped her out, and woke Skeet up. He had stopped a short distance from the homestead, and Maddie was secretly glad – not that Kareena would have got out, but from here it was improbable that she could even see the desolate front garden, let alone the dilapidated condition of the house itself. Maddie did not want any more of that patronization, and for once she was grateful that Steve had seemed to read her mind, with that uncanny knack he had.

'Well, feller,' Steve ruffled Skeet's hair, 'have a good week-end, and keep up that football. Goodbye, Madeleine.'

'Goodbye. Thank you for bringing me home.'

He grinned.

'If I thought you meant that, I'd tell you it was no trouble at all,' he replied blandly, before he walked away back to his car.

Seconds later, Maddie heard him changing gear as he gathered speed along the road. There was no doubt that he and Kareena made a handsome picture, sitting together in that great big car. They all went well together – the car, and Steve, and Kareena.

Maddie shrugged her shoulders irritably. The thought had made her feel oddly sore and miserable inside, she did not know why. Probably because she was tired, and too hot, and had found their enforced company a strain, she supposed. She put all thoughts of them firmly out of her head, and walked resolutely into the house.

The week-end was spent, generally speaking, in indulging Skeet as before. Maddie admitted that it was some weakness in herself which allowed her to do it, and that probably it was bad for Skeet in the long run, but she also had the idea that he would only be young once, and that there were a lot of things lacking in his life – things like a father and mother, for instance, and a nice little home instead of this rambling and comfortless place. Maddie wanted to make up to him for the lack of all those things that she longed to give him but was powerless to acquire, and at times she felt almost hopeless with an all-pervading sense of inadequacy and frustration.

After Skeet had returned to school again, she started to paint the inside of the house. She had ordered some white paint through the mailman, and now she began to cover the ugly caramel colour which seemed to be everywhere she looked, and which she found depressing in the extreme. It was useless even to consider replacing the outside paint. It was in such a peeling condition that it would need to be removed professionally, she felt sure.

She started in the hall, and by the end of the week had worked her way through to the kitchen. The following week saw the completion of that, and also the adjacent boiler-room and meathouse. Maddie was pleased with her handiwork, and Skeet, when he came home, was encouraging, too.

'Golly, Mad! What a difference! It's beginning to look quite – quite *homey*, isn't it!'

Maddie could have hugged him for his choice of adjective, even if it wasn't the kind one found in recognized dictionaries. 'Homey' was what she wanted to make this unloved unlived-in homestead, above all else, and 'homey' was what Skeet had said.

In between times she practised her driving, wishing that she had been able to have a second round of instruction from Tom, for she realized that she had still a great deal to learn before she could be classed as proficient.

Tom had rung her up once or twice on the phone, and she had had several long and entertaining conversations with him. His father had had to go away again, but when he returned, Tom would have more time to spare, and the first thing he intended to do, he told Maddie, was to come out and see her again – unless she could get in to town? His mother had enjoyed her company, and would love to have her for the day again at any time – she must just say when would suit her, and he would arrange it.

Maddie told him, in turn, about the painting, and how much nicer the house was looking, and how Skeet had said it was 'homey'.

'Well, don't fall off the ladder, or something, Maddie, will you? I'll ring you about the end of the week. So long, sweetie.'

'So long.'

When the telephone rang towards the middle of the week, and Maddie put down her paint brush carefully and went to answer, she naturally thought it would be Tom. However, when the operator said 'Long distance calling', amid a series of buzzing noises, she realized that it couldn't be Tom after all, and she was at a complete loss as to who could possibly be phoning her.

It was with the greatest surprise, and an unprecedented measure of delight, that she heard Robert's voice.

'Maddie? Darling, is that you at last? It's Robert.'

'Robert!' She felt quite dazed at first. 'Rob! Where are you speaking from? It's so good to hear you!'

His voice was distant, but quite distinct. He sounded a very long way away indeed.

'I've been in Brisbane.'

'Brisbane?'

'Yes, Maddie, Brisbane. And listen, Maddie. I'll be passing quite close to Noonday on our roundabout way south again. We've a little job to do, and when I look at the map I see you won't be far away at all. I thought I'd stop off and see you. I'll only have a few hours, but it'd be worth it. I just *have* to see you. There's something I want to tell you, something important.'

'Oh, Rob.' Maddie was trying to collect her thoughts. How could he possibly come out, if he only had a few hours? 'It's sixty miles from Noonday, Rob. It takes just ages to get here.'

Robert thought a moment.

'Well, could you come in, and meet me? I know it's a lot to ask, but there'll be two other men with me, and I can't take them so far out of the way. We're on a tight schedule, you see.'

Maddie hesitated.

'I could try,' she said dubiously.

'Yes, do try. It's important – to me, at any rate. If I don't see you now, Maddie, it might be a whole year, mightn't it, until we see each other again. Can you make it the day after tomorrow?'

Maddie was thinking hard. She was remembering all Robert's kindness, his steadiness and dependability, his help when her morale had been so low, his interest in Skeet, the lovely evening of dancing he had wanted to give her, which had been spoilt by Steve's goddess.

'Yes, I'll come, Robert. I'll be there. At a place called The Royal, in the main street. The day after tomorrow.'

'Bless you, Maddie! 'Bye for now, and be sure to be there, won't you? Don't stand me up!' he laughed, and Maddie smiled, too, at her end of the phone.

'I won't,' she promised. 'I'll be there.'

But *how*? she asked herself, when she had replaced the receiver. How do I get there?

It was the same old problem, but this time it was more difficult to solve, because Tom could not help her out.

Steve? Maddie was reluctant to ask him, but in the present circumstances, she could think of no alternative.

'Of course I'll run you in, Madeleine.' Steve seemed agreeable and willing. 'I'm glad you asked me, if a little surprised that you did. You must want to get to town pretty badly!'

Maddie flushed at his dry tone.

'I've to meet a – er – a friend for lunch,' she said, 'someone I knew in Sydney, who hasn't much time to spare and can't come out here. I'd very much like to see him, but he's just passing through. It would mean a lot to me to see him, Steve, and this is my only chance.'

There was silence at the other end of the line. Then Steve's deep drawl came through again.

'I see,' he said, in that way that made Maddie feel too transparent for words. 'Well, in that case, Madeleine, I'm at your disposal. As a matter of fact, Kareena can use a trip to town, too, so we'll make a day of it.'

The receiver clicked down.

Maddie stood by the wall and sighed. Another journey with Kareena was not an especially attractive thought, but she'd put up with anything to repay Robert for some of his kindness to her!

When the time came, she found she could not wear her little two-piece again, because there was a mark, like a grease-stain, near the hem. She would need to use a solvent to remove it, and as she had none at Yattabilla, there was nothing for it but to put on her emerald shift – the one she had worn the very first time she had met Steve in Mr. Opal's office.

She felt at an immediate disadvantage when she reached the car and found Kareena there, impeccably turned out in an expensive shantung costume, with crocodile bag and shoes. She was perfect, she really was! Maddie admitted the fact to herself in a generous spurt of honesty. There was absolutely no flaw visible in either Kareena or her attire, and Maddie reflected on the imbalance of a Fate which could endow one person alone with so many enviable qualities. It was hardly fair! The odd thing was, though, that even with all her many advantages, Kareena did not seem to be a happy person. Her lovely mouth pouted more than it smiled, and her eyes chose to be cold and critical more often than to be warm and friendly. Or perhaps it was just because of Maddie's own presence that she chose to be so petulant. No doubt she regarded Maddie as a nuisance, but she might have acted a little more graciously, since Steve had said that she, too, could use a trip into town, mightn't she!

Beyond a coldly formal greeting, Kareena said absolutely nothing to Maddie the whole way into town. Steve, too, was strangely silent, except to say 'Thank you, Madeleine' when she opened the gates, like he had the last time.

Steve insisted on her having some morning tea with them upon arrival, after which she was thankful to escape, excusing herself by saying she had some shopping to do.

'We'll meet here again about five o'clock, then, Madeleine, if that's all right with you? I promised Mrs. Farrell, my housekeeper, that Kareena and I would be back for dinner.'

'Yes, very well, Steve. I shan't keep you waiting.'

Kareena and I – for dinner. What a pleasantly intimate sound that had! Maddie tried to imagine what Bibbi must be like, and what Mrs. Farrell would prepare for her sophisticated guest for dinner. Steve's house sounded so modern and luxurious that perhaps they even dressed for dinner. She could visualize the scene, Kareena statuesque, in one of those deceptively simple dinner-gowns that accentuated her faultless figure, and Steve dark and awesome, suave in his dinner jacket. Maddie found the picture a singularly disturbing one. In fact, she wished that she had never begun to think of it at all! It was no business of hers, anyway.

She bought herself a bottle of cleaning fluid in the store to remove the grease-mark from her suit when she got home, and then wandered about, rather at a loss, until it was time to meet Robert.

When she saw him standing waiting for her outside The Royal, he looked so dear and kind and familiar that Maddie ran across the street and right into his arms. She found herself hugging him like a long-lost brother.

'Oh, Rob! I *am* glad to see you!'

'Maddie!' He held her away from him. 'I was hoping you'd make it, and here you are, as lovely as ever. No, a little on the thin side, darling, but gorgeous, all the same. It's a wonder you haven't melted dead away in this climate, if you ask me. Is it always as beastly hot as this in Noonday?'

Maddie laughed gaily. It was exciting to see Robert again, and here, of all places, so unexpectedly.

'It has been like this ever since I came. You get used to it. Take your jacket off, though, Rob. Everyone else has. Look! Nobody even bothers to wear them for eating out here.'

'Yes, that's certainly better.' He hung his coat on one of the hooks, and placed his hat over it. It was a pork-pie sort of hat, natty and cityfied, and looked somehow out of place beside the rows of wide country felts on either side of it.

'Now, what will you have?' Robert asked her across the table.

'There *is* only one thing,' Maddie informed him, 'and that's steak and eggs. But it's good steak!'

'Two steaks and eggs, please,' Robert said to the waitress. 'I'm told it's good steak, too.'

'It's beaut,' agreed the waitress laconically, and went off to get it.

'Now, Maddie, tell me all you've been doing since you left. How is Skeet? And how are you managing to get along at Yattabilla?'

As they ate, Maddie told him all the things that had happened to her and Skeet since they had come out here into the country. She didn't make it all sound quite so funny as she had to Mrs. Simson, because Robert knew her so well that he would have seen through that sort of bravado. As she talked, his eyes became more grave, and there were signs of tension in his expression.

'I hate to think of you there all by yourself, Maddie,' he said wretchedly. 'In your letter you didn't even mention that Skeet had to live away from home most of the time. I've been missing you and worrying about you as it is, but heaven knows, I'd have been ten times more miserable if I'd known you hadn't even your brother for company. It's a good thing I came by on this trip, or I might never have found out.'

'There didn't seem much point in saying anything, Rob,' Maddie shrugged. 'After all, there's nothing you could have done about it, any more than I could myself. It's just the way things turned out. How *did* you come by, anyway? I do hope you haven't come a long way off your route just to see us?'

'No, I haven't. It was unbelievable luck, as it turned out. The firm has a government contract for several water-schemes they're starting. One was up near Brisbane, and the other, for a dam, is only fifty miles or so north of here. We were to survey it on our way back, and it seemed a heaven-sent opportunity to see you.'

'I see. Does that mean that you'll be coming back again, then?'

'Not me, no. The construction boys will be next on the scene. We've done our part, and they'll act on our findings.'

Maddie spooned the remains of her ice-cream neatly into her mouth. 'And what have you done with the other men who are travelling with you?'

Robert smiled.

'They've gone for a swim, of all things. It seems there's a beaut waterhole down in the river here, and they reckoned it was a good chance to cool off. They'll be hanging around here later in the afternoon – I pointed the place out. I thought you and I could go for a walk somewhere, maybe – somewhere where we could talk. Is there anywhere shady around here?'

She thought for a moment.

'There's a lovely park, where it's nice and cool. We wouldn't have to walk very far, and there are seats under the trees.'

'Spendid.' Robert collected his jacket and put on his hat as they came out into the sun. This time he did not put on his coat, but slung it over one arm, and took Maddie's own arm with his free hand.

Together they strolled over the lawns in the park, down among the trees where the little paddling pool was. There were some ducks there today, and several children were feeding them with crusts of bread which they had brought. It was pleasant watching the tame birds snapping the water as the pieces fell near them, and hearing the children's shrill laughter and exclamations.

Afterwards they found a seat, and talked spasmodically. Robert seemed to be preoccupied, and Maddie was content to leave him to his thoughts, for the afternoon heat, the buzzing of bees in the flower-beds behind them, the distant voices and floating laughter of the children, all had a soporific effect on her.

It was Robert who finally broke the silence.

'Maddie, you said a while ago, at lunch, that there was nothing I could do about you having to live there at Yattabilla all alone. And, if you remember, I had already told you on the phone that I had something to say that was important. Well, the two things are directly linked. There *is* something I can do, and it's something I want very much – something that I hope you will want as much as I do. I want you to marry me, Maddie.'

Maddie looked at him, drawing her breath swiftly. Her eyes felt as if they must be as round as a couple of saucers.

'Will you, Maddie? Please? I can see I've taken you by surprise, but I've given it a great deal of thought, and it's what I want to do most in the whole world. I've missed you dreadfully since you left, and it would solve your problem for you, too.'

She gazed at him in a dazed fashion. Such a thought as marriage had never entered her head, and here was Robert, asking her to enter that very state.

She liked Robert – liked him enormously. Why, then, was she not feeling breathlessly ecstatic at his proposal? What was the matter with her? Why couldn't she fling herself into his arms, and say 'Yes, yes, yes, oh, Robert, yes, please.' That's what Maddie would have liked to do! That's what she wished she *could* do, only something was holding her back. She couldn't understand what was happening inside her, but it was as if a great truth was crystallizing itself somewhere in the region of her heart. Maddie could not tell what the truth was going to be, just yet. She would have to wait for her heart to send a message to her mind – a sort of translatory message, it would need to be – to tell her what this torn, unhappy, incredible feeling could mean.

What was she to say to Robert? Dear Robert, sitting there watching her in the most puzzled, uncertain way.

'But, Rob,' she heard her shaken voice utter doubtfully, 'one can't get married just to – well, to solve a *problem*.'

'Maddie! It isn't *only* that! That's only a part of it – a very small part.' Robert took her hand, looked down at her fingers curled in his. 'I love you, you see. I thought I could wait a year, and now I know I can't. It's impossible, knowing you're there alone at that miserable Yattabilla. I had meant to wait, I'll admit that. I meant to wait until my prospects improved, so that I could offer you and Skeet much more than I can at the moment, but the fact is, Maddie, that almost anything will be better for you than what you have *now*. Come back to Sydney with me – you and Skeet. Throw up this crazy residence thing, and come back with me, and let me take care of you both. Marry me, please, Maddie?'

Robert was so humble, so persuasive. Maddie felt dreadful, because she knew she was going to have to hurt this person whom she liked very much. The blinding force within her had taken control of her actions, even though it had not yet identified itself to her. It was making her say things she didn't really want to say at all.

'Rob, my dear, I can't. I am so very sorry, but I can't.'

'Why not?'

'Because – I – I – don't know why, but I just know it wouldn't work out.'

'I'd make it work out,' insisted Robert confidently.

'No, Rob, you couldn't, and neither could I. It wouldn't be right from the very beginning. I can see that now. I – I don't love you in the *right* way, Robert.'

He took her other hand, patiently.

'Darling, that would come,' he told her gently. 'I don't expect you to feel the same as I do, not at first, but you would grow to love me. Loving someone is a sort of togetherness, really. We'd be together all the time, and your love would grow.'

'No, Rob.' She was sad, but adamant.

'Maddie, *why*?'

'Dear, I've told you. I've done my best to explain.'

Robert looked at her thoughtfully.

'And I can't accept your explanation, Maddie. It's too negative. There's no positive reason why—' He broke off, tensing suddenly. 'Maddie, there's no one else, is there?' he asked anxiously. 'Is there someone else?'

'No, of course not, Rob!' said Maddie, but even as she said it, even as she looked straight into Robert's dear, kind face and said those words, she saw his features change. The eyes she was gazing into were not Robert's at all! They were clear, grey, penetrating eyes, that could be uncomfortably intent one minute, infinitely tender the next. They were fine, steady, proud eyes, and the black brows above them could draw together quickly into a quite terrifying scowl, or they could lift satirically, or quirk with humour. Steve! Oh, *Steve*!

'Maddie? Darling, are you all right? You look as if you'd seen a ghost, you're so pale!' Robert was back. He was sitting on the seat beside her, shaking her gently, anxiously.

'I'm – all right,' she managed to falter.

A ghost? If only Robert had been right!

To be haunted by a ghost presented no problems – at least, not when you compared it with being haunted by a real, live, virile man, who not only lived on the very next property, but was the trustee of your father's estate as well.

Maddie was thoroughly staggered, utterly aghast at herself. How could she love Steve, when she knew that she hated him? Love? Hate? How closely allied those two emotions must be she was only now discovering, because Maddie had known for the last few minutes what the great, secret truth was that her heart had been harbouring. That truth was that she loved the very man that she had thought she hated. She loved Steve Darley with every fibre of her being, with an all-consuming dedication that was as hopeless as it was unrequited.

Oh, Steve!

'My dear, we'll have to go.' Robert glanced at his watch, pulled her gently to her feet. 'I've kept you too long as it is, in this heat. Between that and the surprise, you've been knocked sideways.' He stood looking down at her, still patient and considerate. 'We won't say any more about it just now, not if it upsets you. But think about it, darling. I want you to think about it very carefully, and then write to me. Will you?'

'It's no good, Robert,' she said dully.

'Do it all the same, will you? For me? I'm not going to give up as easily as all that!'

'I'll – I'll try,' she agreed weakly.

'Promise?'

'Yes, I promise.'

'You're still awfully pale. We'll walk back slowly. You've been doing too much – all that painting and everything.' He sounded stern and disapproving.

Maddie stumbled along at his side, too miserable and confused to talk.

As they neared the Royal, two men in a parked car gave a signal toot. They were waiting there to collect Robert, obviously. Further down the street, on the same side, Maddie could see Steve's big Chev. He and Kareena were sitting in it, but when he saw Maddie coming, he opened his door and got out, stretching in a leisurely way in the hot sun.

Maddie dragged at Robert's sleeve.

'Let's say goodbye here, Rob,' she whispered a little desperately. She held out her hand.

Robert took her hand and then, before she knew what he intended to do, he had pulled her into his arms, and was giving her a quick, fierce kiss.

'I love you so much, Maddie,' he muttered into her hair. 'Promise to think about what I said?'

'Oh, Robert.' She found she was clinging to him with a mixture of guilt and compassion, hardly knowing what she did. 'I'll write, I truly will.'

'And try to make it yes.' He kissed her again, briefly and gently.

The next moment Robert was getting into the car with his companions, and Maddie was walking numbly towards Steve, standing nonchalantly beside his rear passenger door. He opened it for her, and she felt his eyes boring into her uncomfortably. Maddie found that she couldn't look at him – she just stared fixedly ahead of her, at nothing.

When he took her upper arm in a firm grasp, she shook herself free almost frenziedly.

'Take it easy, Madeleine, and get in there, for God's sake,' he drawled softly right into her ear. 'It's a heart-rending farewell for you, no doubt, but you don't want to make a fool of yourself right here in the street, do you?'

Maddie was aware that she was still standing there

woodenly. A glance at Steve's set face was enough to set her scrambling into the car with almost hysterical haste.

His grey eyes, which could sometimes surprise her with gentleness, were as cold and forbidding as she had ever seen them!

CHAPTER NINE

THE next few days were ones of rainy weather.

It wasn't even crisp, refreshing sort of rain, thought Maddie sourly, as she went about the house mopping up pools of water and placing basins at strategic intervals beneath the worst of the drips. Rather was it a steady, dismal drizzle – as dismal as her own thoughts. It kept Skeet more or less confined to the house at the week-end, and when the school bus called for him on Monday it came churning up the track in a flurry of black mud. Maddie was amazed at the way that arid, hard-baked plain could soften into dark mudpans when it became soaked with water. She waved goodbye to Skeet, standing clear of the spray as the bus's wheels spun aimlessly for a moment, then took a grip of firmer ground beneath them.

By the next morning the sky had cleared, and things began to dry up. Maddie, who had been painting away at those horrid, flaking caramel walls all the time she had been indoors, was glad to see a pale, sultry sun struggling through once more. Steam rose off the flat down near the creek, and there was a strange tangy smell off the rain-soaked gum-leaves.

In the afternoon, she thought she would practise driving the car again. Carefully she reversed it from the garage – she was always thankful when that bit was safely over! – and took a few tentative turns around the homestead. Gaining confidence, she headed down the track a little way. There was a wide turning place about half a mile down the road, where she could sweep right around in one go without having to back and fill. Tom had not taught her how to do that yet.

Maddie was never sure, afterwards, just what went wrong, or how she slipped into that skid. One moment she was accelerating confidently, with her front wheels aligned perfectly with the road ahead. The next, one tyre seemed to drop into the mud-soft earth shoulder at one side, and she was being dragged off the road. When she tried to steer her way back, she only gathered speed as the car got out of control.

Too late, she recollected that one is supposed to drive *into* a skid. She saw the bunch of trees looming in front of her, but was powerless to alter her course. Even as she spun the wheel frantically right into the line the car was taking, she realized that she had acted too late. She would have been better to brake and stop altogether, as it turned out, because the Buick was headed dead on course for those trees, and was in fact going quite fast when it hit the nearest one.

There was a sickening crash. Maddie felt herself flung into the air, and for some panic-stricken moments seemed to hurtle through an endless space. Then there was an explosion of pain in her head, and after that, total darkness.

She had no means of knowing just how long she lay there. It might only have been minutes, it could have been hours.

Her first awareness was of the wrecked car, some yards off, and then of the steamy sunlight beating down on her. Gingerly she moved her legs, one after the other. They seemed all right, although her whole body felt bruised and battered. When she came to move her left arm, though, pain brought perspiration to her brow, and she lay back, quite still, not daring to stir again until it had receded.

Lying there, collecting herself, Maddie became aware of something she had not noticed before. On the skyline, up there on the ridge, was the silhouette of a horseman, just behind the two clumps of trees that were the monster's ears. Both man and beast were completely motionless, and the rider's form was leaning forward against the animal's neck. They must have been there for some time, and Maddie thought to herself that it could only be Steve.

She had never known she could be so relieved at the

knowledge that another human being was around! She needed help, no doubt about that, and even Steve would be a godsend right now. She'd have to try to attract his attention.

Painfully and slowly she raised herself to a sitting position, and waved her right arm. She was stiff and sore, and movement brought unwelcome jabs of pain in its wake, but it was necessary, all the same. She waved again, and still the profiled figure remained immobile. It didn't even wave back. Then, to Maddie's horror and disbelief, she saw it begin to move away – not down this side of the ridge, the Yattabilla side, towards her, but in the opposite direction!

She struggled to her feet, mindless of the stiffness, and waved and even shouted, but the dark figure only got smaller and smaller. The next moment it had dropped down out of sight on the other side of the horizon.

Maddie stared at the place where the horse and rider had disappeared, trying to take in the fact that they had gone. Steve had gone! He had actually gone away and left her, lying – or rather, sitting – in the mud beside a bashed-up car! Maybe he had actually left her here on purpose, to die. If she were dead, he would get Yattabilla, wouldn't he? she thought grimly. And what a nice easy way in which to get it. You simply rode off and left your adversary to *die*!

Indignation, sheer downright rage enveloped Maddie. She was far from dead, as he would soon find out! A little bit hurt, maybe. That arm was a bit of a bother, and there was a swelling on her temple where she had hit her head, but neither was the type of injury that was likely to kill anyone! Poor Steve, he would soon discover that he was out of luck, if that was what he hoped.

Maddie began to make her way slowly homeward. She shuffled along, aching in every joint, and it took her an interminable time to reach the house. She staggered over the verandah and into the hall, then lurched along to the bathroom, where she made a half-hearted attempt to remove the mud from her bare legs. Her cotton dress was torn and stained, and the face that gazed back at her from the mirror was paper-white, except for the dust which had mingled with perspiration in grimy streaks, and the blood-caked contusion at the side of her head.

Maddie supposed it *must* be her face, since there was nobody else here at Yattabilla homestead who could be looking into that mirror. It looked pretty awful, but it would have to wait. She felt too shaken and exhausted to do more just now. Indeed, it was with the greatest measure of relief that she gained her bedroom and lay down gingerly on top of her bed.

She smiled bitterly to herself. She was for all the world like a wounded animal which crawls back to its lair to nurse its injuries alone.

She drifted into a state of semi-shock, almost of stupor, to be aroused a short time later by the sound of heavy footsteps outside. They took the verandah steps in a couple of bounds, and came quickly into the hall. The next second Steve had burst into the room.

'Madeleine? Are you here? Well, thank God for that! I've been searching everywhere!' His face as he approached the bed was pale and stern beneath the tan, and his eyes snapped with a mixture of anger and relief.

'I'm here, and I'm all right,' she mumbled. 'Please leave me alone.'

'You're not fit to be left alone – in more ways than one!' he barked irately. 'What the hell do you think you were playing at, trying to drive that ramshackle old car when you haven't even a clue how the thing works?'

He sounded unbelievably furious, and Maddie was stung to life.

'I *have* got a clue,' she retorted with spirit, 'and I *do* know how it works. Tom gave me some lessons.'

'I thought as much,' Steve ground out, between clenched teeth. 'The senseless young idiot! He might have guessed you'd try it out alone!'

'I've been practising for weeks,' she told him indignantly.

'I'm getting quite good at it, too. It was only today that something went wrong.'

'Wrong! You hit that tree with one hell of a smack, by the condition of the wreckage! How d'you think I felt, hunting around out there with not a sign of you anywhere? You might have killed yourself. As it is, you seem to be all in one piece, thank heaven!'

He bent over her, and Maddie could have sworn that there was anxiety in his intent look – that is, if she hadn't already known that he had ridden away on purpose and left her to die! The hypocrite, she thought confusedly, because his nearness was bringing on a sort of mental panic.

'Let's see what damage you've managed to do, all the same.'

Steve put out a hand, and Maddie shrunk away. Unaccountably, she had begun to shiver.

'Don't you *touch* me, Steve Darley!' she shrilled through teeth that chattered. 'Don't you dare!'

Her eyes defied him, halted him momentarily in his intentions. He just stood there looking down at her thoughtfully, and then he tried again. There was a new, patient note in his voice this time.

'Come on, Madeleine,' he said reasonably. 'I'll be gentle, I promise, but we have to know, don't we? Maybe you do know already. Maybe you could just tell me, eh?'

His deep, coaxing tone was almost too much for Maddie. It brought tears to her eyes and a wobble to her own voice.

'What do you care?' she quavered almost unintelligibly. 'You rode away.'

'I – what?' He sounded incredulous.

'You rode away. You went *away*, on your horse. You left me!' She was almost crying, she was so distraught. 'Maybe you didn't think I saw you up there on the ridge, on your horse. You were looking right down on me, so you must have seen me, too. And then when I waved, you went away. I waved and waved, I even called, but you rode away!'

Steve stared down at her all the time she was speaking. His face had been expressionless all that time. Not even a single, flitting pang of guilt crossed his features for a moment. Only when she stopped did a shade of warmth enter those cold grey eyes, and slowly, to her amazement, she watched it spread into a look of great kindness and compassion.

He shook his head slowly, and a small smile lifted one corner of his grim mouth.

'I didn't ride away and leave you, Madeleine,' he told her very gently. 'The man you saw up there on the ridge was Billy Sundown. He's one of my stockmen, although I can't expect that you'd have realized that. When he saw you move beside the wrecked car, he came home to tell me, and that was the right thing for him to do. He knew it was something for his boss to handle. I didn't come over on horseback myself, I came in the car, because I had a feeling it would be needed. It's just outside.' He paused, leaned over her. '*Now* will you let me inspect the damage?'

Maddie was beyond words, but in any case Steve didn't wait for a reply. She closed her eyes as she felt his hands moving quickly over her bruised limbs, as expert and impersonal as any doctor's.

'That's fine.' Satisfied so far, he held up her right wrist. 'This has had a nasty wrench. Let me see you move your fingers.'

Maddie wiggled them obediently in his own hard, work-toughened ones.

'No break there,' he said on a note of relief, 'although we'll have it X-rayed just in case. The main trouble seems to be this other arm.'

He lifted it gently, but even that cautious movement made Maddie gasp with pain. She seemed to be drowning in that unpleasant sensation. Steve's face hovered above her, dimmed and receded, as she drifted off on a pain-racked cloud.

When she came to, there was a welcome feeling of

coolness about her face, and a deep voice spoke very near her hair.

'Lie still, darling,' it said. Or rather, that's what Maddie imagined that it had said. She must still be drifting in that cloud of semi-consciousness to even think such a thing!

She opened her eyes to find that Steve was wiping her face, very gently, with a soft cold cloth. He was wiping away the blood and dust marks. The pain had gone, and her left arm was in an improvised sling, strapped firmly against her body.

'Better?' Steve's own face was pale and set. It seemed an effort for him to summon up the faint, reassuring grin he gave her. 'You've broken your collar-bone, Madeleine, and I'm going to take you in to the hospital to get fixed up. After that you're coming back to Bibbi with me.'

Maddie stared. She still felt vague, and it was difficult to take in what he was saying.

'I can't,' she reminded him in a husky whisper. 'Don't you remember, Steve? I can't. I have to stay at Yattabilla. That's what Mr. Opal said.'

Steve looked impatient.

'My dear girl, Mr. Opal would be the first to agree that the legal aspect be held in abeyance, under the circumstances,' he told her tersely. 'I'm not leaving you here alone in your present condition, so let's call a temporary truce, shall we? I'm going to get you a small cup of tea and a couple of tablets I've got in the car, and from then on you'll do as I say. I'm in no mood to argue, so be warned.'

Maddie respected that warning!

As she sipped the tea he brought her, and obediently swallowed the tablets, she could see that it would be dangerous to oppose Steve in his present mood. Gone was the gentleness which she knew she had not dreamed, even though that tender 'darling' had been a figment of her imagination. Now there was only impatience to be gone – that, and the physical frustration which enforced inaction at a sickbed can cause in a big, active man like Steve.

Impatience and frustration were in every movement of his powerful frame as he walked about the room with his hands in his pockets while Maddie drank her tea. He was like a half-tamed tiger, resentful of its confinement. When she had finished her drink, he took the cup from her, set it on the bedside table, and pulled open the drawers in the dressing-chest. Then he took her dressing-gown from the hook behind the door, and began to fling things into the canvas hold-all with masculine abandon.

'You can tell me if I miss out on any essentials,' he said grimly. 'You don't need much. Pyjamas? Nightdress? Whatever it is, where is it?'

'There's a clean one in my bottom drawer, and my sponge-bag is in the bathroom,' Maddie replied with meek apology, aware that he was anxious to be gone. She felt a dreadful nuisance, and a bit of a traitor, too. Steve *hadn't* ridden away and left her, after all! It had been Billy Sundown, the grizzled aboriginal stockman she had once seen in town, who had watched her on the ridge, and who had then gone away to tell his boss. She hoped it was not the fact that she had accused Steve of riding off and leaving her that made him look so grim and tense just now. She was sorry she had misjudged him – she really was. Sorry *and* glad. She was glad that her suspicions had turned out to be unwarranted!

Maddie slid her legs over the end of the bed and found herself caught neatly by Steve, and lifted carefully into his arms. She was thankful to rest her head against his shirt, because nausea had suddenly assailed her at the movement of her bruised body when she stood up.

'Stubborn little thing, aren't you?' Steve's voice chided her, and then, as he took in the whiteness about her mouth, he put his head down closer, adding, 'I'm sorry, Madeleine. I'll try not to jolt you.'

Maddie felt his lips brushing her forehead, his face was so near to hers. Of course it was a purely accidental contact, because when she raised her eyes his expression was as unrevealing as usual, and that meant he had not even been aware that his mouth had brushed over her brow with a touch as light and fleeting as a butterfly's.

He put her gently into the back seat and placed a cushion behind her head.

'Would you rather lie right down? No? Hold tight then, for a quick trip into town.'

Steve hardly spoke the whole way into Noonday. As they passed the smashed Buick, leaning crazily up against a stout apple-gum, you could have cut the silence with a knife. Soon after that Steve groped in his shirt pocket for the makings, and rolled himself a cigarette. Maddie, from her half-reclining position in the back seat, admired the dexterity with which he managed to do that and at the same time maintain a steady driving speed.

When he left her at the hospital, he smiled at her. It was the first real smile he had given her since the moment he came storming into her room to find her.

'Well, Madeleine, here goes! They're going to keep you in overnight just to make sure there's no concussion. They'll see you get a good rest, too, and I'll come in the morning to take you home.'

Home? Home to Bibbi, he meant. *His* home, certainly, but one that could never be hers. The thought was so painful, her longing and love for him so great, that Maddie wondered how she was going to be able to bear being there at Bibbi, with Steve. And with Kareena. She had almost forgotten about Kareena!

She smiled in return, gamely.

'Thank you, Steve. And thank you for bringing me here. I – I'm sorry,' she said inadequately. What she really meant was that she was sorry for thinking he had ridden off to leave her to die, when he had instead been kind and efficient and even quite gentle in between his bouts of anger and exasperation.

Steve glanced down at her wan face, at her pluckily

smiling mouth. He grinned, and ruffled her hair in the same way he sometimes did with Skeet, just as if she had been a child.

'I'll be back in the morning, Madeleine.'

He walked out of the ward then, with that long easy stride, leaving Maddie to the ministrations of the doctor and nurses.

When he came back the next day, Maddie was sitting in a chair beside her bed, waiting for him.

Even in his faded moleskins and khaki shirt, and carrying that battered wide-brimmed hat, he looked carelessly handsome. Maddie could smell a clean shaving-lotion smell as he bent to pick up her bag.

'I can walk today,' she assured him quickly. 'I'm feeling much, much better. A bit stiff and sore, but it will soon wear off. I – er – I can't see any real need to come to Bibbi, Steve, can you? Couldn't you just drop me off at Yattabilla again?'

'No, Madeleine, I could not,' he replied firmly. 'I've had a report on you from the doctor, and you're to take things easy for the next week. There's a distinct possibility of delayed shock, and he advises bed most of the time, with increasing exercise as the days go on. O.K.?'

Maddie sighed. 'O.K.,' she agreed resignedly.

She was treated to a penetrating stare.

'What's the matter? You'll *like* Bibbi, I promise you. I'll even keep out of your way if that will make you feel happier. Oh, yes, I've noticed how you go to the most extraordinary lengths to avoid my unwelcome presence!'

'It's not that,' she muttered miserably, with heightened colour.

'What, then? If it's the legal side that bothers you, I've been in touch with Opal and put him in the picture. Will you accept my word on that?'

'Yes, of course!' she said in quick distress. She knew, too late, that she could trust Steve. She could trust him with anything, even with her life, and it hurt her to think that she could ever have doubted him when she loved him so over-whelmingly.

'Right-o, then. Stop looking as though you're going off to the guillotine, and buck up, there's a good girl. Mrs. Farrell is longing to have someone to nurse and spoil!'

Maddie followed him in silence to the car. She offered to open the gates when they came to them, but was unsurprised when Steve would not permit it.

It was strange not to be taking the right-hand fork when they reached the turn-off to Yattabilla, stranger still to be running along the west side of the mountain ridge.

Maddie could see Bibbi homestead from a long way off. It crouched on the plain ahead of them, backed by ornamental trees and lawns, succoured by a pumped water supply from the nearby Barron Creek. The house itself was white, in the old colonial style with handsome pillars at the front, and creeping vines of wistaria and bougainvillea. There were so many other buildings of varying sizes round about it that to Maddie's innocent gaze it looked more like a small village than a station homestead. All the outhouses had white corrugated roofs, and on the far side, away from the rest, was a low, more recent building with a windsock drooping motionless nearby. That must be the hangar where Steve kept his plane, she supposed.

The avenue up which they now drove was lined with several different species of pine and the odd pepper-tree. Momentarily, as they encountered the deep shade of the overhanging boughs, the house was lost to view, and then suddenly they were upon it, with the lawns which she had seen from the distance now on either side of the sweep of gravel, and flowerbeds making gay borders wherever she looked.

Maddie thought that she would remember for ever her first view of Bibbi homestead, but Steve appeared to be oblivious to the magnificence about him. He helped her out, and introduced her to the kindly Mrs. Farrell, who had come down the steps to meet them, then he took her case to her room, while she and the housekeeper followed more slowly.

Soon she was tucked between hem-stitched linen sheets in a cool, airy bedroom of palatial proportions. Her windows looked out on to boxes of petunias, and beyond those the trees and lawns stretched in a green and peaceful backdrop.

Maddie spent the first few days drowsing pleasantly, and reading the magazines that Mrs. Farrell had put at her bedside. She made herself walk about her room and into the adjoining tiled bathroom, knowing that action was the only remedy for her strained and aching muscles.

Steve came to see her every day, politely inquiring after her health. Apart from that, he left her alone. Maddie supposed he must be with Kareena. She had not seen Kareena at all, but she knew that she was there, because Mrs. Farrell sometimes included her name in the conversation. Miss Powell, she called her.

When Friday morning came, Steve told her that he had arranged for the bus to leave Skeet off at Bibbi instead of Yattabilla.

Maddie protested. 'I think we should go home,' she said. 'I can't go on trespassing on your hospitality like this. I feel a fraud!'

Steve smiled kindly.

'You've no need to feel that way, Madeleine. I can assure you that you aren't at all in the way, and Mrs. Farrell is enjoying herself enormously. You'll stay until next Friday, and then, if you like, you can go back to Yattabilla in time for Skeet's bus.'

'I'm perfectly recovered. Truly.' She wanted desperately to get away from Bibbi. Why, with Skeet here too, they'd be almost like a family! It hurt to even think of it!

Steve came closer. Just for a moment he cupped her face between his palms and inspected the bump on her temple. He ran his fingers over the swelling with a touch that was incredibly light for such large, masculine hands.

'Not perfectly,' he corrected, 'not yet. But I'll tell you what. From tomorrow you can live more normally, to the extent you're able with that arm supported like that. Mrs. Farrell will still help you to bathe and dress, but you'll take your meals with Kareena and me. That will be nicer for Skeet, too.'

Skeet certainly seemed to enjoy himself that week-end. Steve took him swimming in the pool, and helped him to catch several small carp in the creek with the aid of a home-made line. The child made friends with the Bibbi hens, too, and when he told Steve that he was worried about Etta, Steve laughed and said not to be, that he had told Mrs. Lawrence to look after the poultry again in the meantime.

Mrs. Farrell welcomed Skeet, too, as warmly as she had his sister. She treated him with just the right balance of firmness and maternal indulgence, and Skeet responded to this approach.

'I like Mrs. Farrell, Maddie,' he confided. 'Even when she's angry with you, she doesn't really get narky, an' she always tells you *why* – not like Kareena,' he added darkly. 'She's angry all the time, I think. Even when she smiles, her eyes don't, not like Mrs. Farrell's that go all laughy. I hate the way Kareena looks at us!'

Maddie knew just what he meant. She was surprised at Skeet's perception, but she could not help agreeing with what he had said. Kareena did not seem to like Skeet any more than she cared for Maddie, and she made no effort to hide the fact from the two people concerned.

At meal times she gave her attention to Steve alone, care-ful to keep the conversation on topics upon which neither Maddie nor Skeet could add so much as a sentence. Personal things, between herself and Steve. She would use all her considerable charm and attraction to hold his full attention, as if he and she were in an intimate little world of their own, choosing for the most part to ignore the other two. When Steve did attempt to draw them into the conversation, Maddie couldn't help noticing how quick and skilful she was at creating a diversion, and making herself the central figure of interest again.

Once she said to Maddie, who had been telling something that was making Steve laugh, 'Will you *please* tell your dear little brother to keep his feet to himself when he's at the dinner-table?'

She said it with an exaggeratedly bored patience, as though it were a nuisance with which she had been putting-up in silence until it was no longer bearable, and Maddie could guess, from the indignant pout on Skeet's red face, that he had done nothing at all – or if he had, that it had been a purely accidental contact.

Another time, Skeet had splashed her linen dress as he came out of the pool, and she exclaimed, 'Look what he's done! You *nasty* little boy! I'll be glad when you're back at school!'

'So will I,' confessed Skeet morosely to Maddie, after that incident. 'I don't like it here with her, even if the rest of the place *is* smashing!'

'Never mind, darling. You'll be off again in the morning, and next week-end we'll be back at Yattabilla.'

Maddie herself was secretly longing for the day. Here she was under a continual mental strain, frightened that by word or deed or look, she might give away the secret that she carried in her heart – her fruitless love for the owner of Bibbi.

That her latent fear had indeed been justified was borne out the day before she was to leave. Maddie was reading in bed before putting her light out for the night, when a brief knock sounded on her door, and before she could even call 'Come in,' Kareena had opened it, slipped into the room, and shut it softly behind her again.

She came over purposefully and sat down on the end of Maddie's bed, beautiful beyond description in an aqua-marine nightdress and matching negligée, with a froth of lace at throat and wrists. Her dark hair fell free beneath her shoulders, and her smooth skin looked like warmed honey in the glow of the bedside light.

'You're leaving tomorrow, aren't you?' she asked without preamble.

'Yes, in the morning.'

Maddie blinked. What a strange thing to ask, at this hour, when the whole household had retired for the night, and she herself might just as easily have been fast asleep as reading a book! Surely Kareena would not have gone to the length of waking her to say that?

It soon became clear that Kareena would go to quite extraordinary lengths to say what was in her mind.

'I thought so,' she said calmly. 'That's why I chose to come tonight. You may feel embarrassed at what I'm going to say, Madeleine, and we'll find it easier on both sides if we don't see each other in the morning. I shall make a special point of sleeping in.' She permitted herself a faint smile.

Maddie felt a chill of premonition playing over her spine. 'Yes?' she prompted, wide-eyed, inwardly steeling herself against the unpleasantness she guessed was to come, although what form it might take she could not even hazard.

'*Don't* be tempted to go out of your depth, my dear, will you?' begged Kareena, then, on an insipidly kind, it's-for-your-own-good sort of note, 'About Steve, I mean,' she elucidated, taking in the other girl's blank stare. 'I know that older, experienced men like Steve can have an almost fatal attraction for young, untried girls like you, but you'd never be able to cope, Madeleine, take it from me. Experience requires experience, you know. I can only urge you to stick to those other nice young men you have – Tom Simson, for one – I don't think I ever knew the other's name, did I?' She gestured vaguely.

Maddie was horror-struck, agonizingly embarrassed and outraged. She put her hands up to her burning cheeks.

'But I – I've *never*—' she began protestingly, when Kareena stopped her.

'Madeleine, there's no need for pretence with me,' she interrupted firmly. 'A woman always knows, especially about another woman's feelings. I can see you're deeply infatuated with Steve – you've been going about like a lovesick adolescent all week. There are all the signs, and I know I'm not mistaken. Just one little point, though, may help you to rid yourself of this ridiculous adulation, and that is –' she paused, regarding her painted nails with interest, knowing that that pause would lend added weight to what was to follow – 'that Steve doesn't happen to be on the books. He's committed already, you see. You don't think he'd have invited me up here out of the social season if he hadn't wanted to ask me something rather special, do you?'

'I – I hadn't thought about it at all,' Maddie heard herself stammer miserably.

'Well, it's time you *did*,' returned Kareena tartly. 'It's high time you *did* think, Madeleine. You really are being rather thoughtless and selfish about the whole thing, aren't you? I mean, Steve didn't ask to have a – a sort of ward foisted on him, did he? That's all he regards you as, you know – a responsibility, and one he can't get rid of for a whole year. Being a gentleman, and loyal, Steve wouldn't put it as bluntly as that to you, but I feel *I* must, because, quite frankly, you are holding up our personal plans. Until Steve relinquishes that wretched trusteeship we can't get married. I intend to have a long honeymoon, perhaps even a trip around the world. Six months, anyway, at the very least, and we can't do that until this tiresome Yattabilla affair is settled. Surely it's a bit much, if, in addition to this inconvenience, you intend to embarrass us by a rather distasteful display of quite unwanted and rather stupid youthful affection.'

'Please go,' Maddie said coldly. She must keep her dignity at all costs. 'Please leave now, Kareena. You've said quite enough.'

Kareena rose gracefully, a tall, willow-slim, elegant goddess.

'I intended to, in any case.' She walked to the door. 'Think over what I've said, won't you, Madeleine?'

Maddie heard the soft click of the knob, and Kareena was gone.

CHAPTER TEN

THINK it over, Kareena had said.

Maddie did indeed think it over! In fact, she tossed and turned miserably right through the night, unable to think of anything else.

It was heartbreaking to find yourself in love with a man who regarded you as little more than an inconvenient responsibility – a sort of debt of honour to a dead friend. It was much worse, much more humiliating, to realize that your secret had been discovered by a ruthless type like Kareena, who would not hesitate to use her knowledge for her own ends.

She had been antagonistic to Maddie from the very start, antagonistic and patronizing. Now her feeling had developed into one of cold hatred which she did not attempt to conceal from Maddie herself, although she was skilful enough at keeping it from Steve. Kareena obviously realized that an open declaration of war would place Steve in a compromising position with his – what was the word Kareena had used? – his ward.

As the hours wore on, and Maddie sweated out her present mental agony, one thing became increasingly clear to her, and that was that, under these new circumstances, she could not suffer to stay at Yattabilla any longer.

What, after all, did the future hold for her there? Supposing she did manage to stick out her year's residence under this dreadful situation – so close to Steve, who could hardly wait to get rid of his responsibility to her, whom she loved with quite shattering singlemindedness, and who was himself betrothed to Kareena Powell.

Even if Maddie stayed, and acquired the Yattabilla property as her inheritance, how could she possibly live there to witness Kareena as the new Mrs. Darley, the mistress of

Bibbi, the love of Steve's life? They would be too tantalizingly near for Maddie ever to begin trying to mend her broken heart, and all the time she would have Kareena's subtle enmity to contend with, as well.

No. To remain at Yattabilla would be unendurable, as well as foolish. It would, in fact, be utterly impossible!

'You'll have to go-away, go-away, go-away,' trilled the bird in the garden outside Maddie's window. Dawn was breaking and she had not managed to snatch even an hour's sleep. Her mind was in a turmoil, seething with uncertain plans for the future. What would she do? Where would she go – she and Skeet? Back to Sydney, obviously, to some dreary, ill-paid job. Thank God she was at least able to support them, after a fashion. She was still independent, and that was something for which to be thankful! Stenography could hardly be termed a glamorous career, but its rewards had always been adequate to keep herself and Skeet.

Skeet! Dear little Skeet! He was at the root of her unhappiness when she thought about the alternatives. He was going to be a sufferer, in so many ways. For the first time in his life, he had tasted a semi-normal existence, with the security of a home behind him, even if that home was a decaying dwelling like the Yattabilla homestead. Maddie knew that, in time, she *could* have made it nice. The white paint was already helping to do that – hadn't Skeet himself declared it 'homey!' – and she had had plans to dig up the garden ground at the front and plant some shrubs and flowers in the autumn.

Now it looked as if they would soon find themselves back in some sort of humble digs in the city, two young individuals lost in the impersonal hurly-burly of urban life. It was a quelling prospect, but one with which Maddie knew she must come to terms.

She had to drag herself out of bed, weary beyond belief. When she looked in the mirror to brush her hair, she saw that her face was a dreadful parchment colour, making the fading bruise on her forehead stand out in liverish contrast.

Her eyes looked back at her, bleak and shadowed.

In the dining-room Steve was breakfasting alone. True to her promise, Kareena had not appeared, and that was something about which to be relieved, Maddie supposed bleakly.

Steve rose to his feet and put her into her chair. He was newly-shaven, and his hair was slicked down tidily, still damp from the shower. Maddie caught the familiar whiff of his after-shave – a masculine aroma that had a curious mixture of tobacco and horses about it, since he was in his everyday, working garb. His muscular brown forearms, with their thick covering of springy hair bleached almost gold by the sun, came down on the arms of her chair on either side, and pushed it nearer the table as she sat down.

Steve took his seat again, and favoured her with a keen regard.

'You don't look well,' he remarked abruptly.

'I'm fine,' she replied with synthetic brightness.

He put out a hand, felt her brow.

'You've been overdoing it. Possibly there's a delayed reaction to the accident, too.' He studied her afresh. 'I think you'd better remain here a few days yet, Madeleine. I'll fetch Skeet from the bus, and he can have another week-end here.'

The mere idea was enough to send Maddie into an almost hysterical panic.

'No, no,' she cried. 'I've got to get back! I *must* get back, today!'

Steve's mobile brow lifted expressively.

'Dear me,' he murmured, 'I'd no idea you were so fervently attached to the place. So be it, then, if you're fretting to be gone.'

That made her feel ungracious.

'It's – not that,' she said unhappily. 'You've been so kind, more than kind, and so has Mrs. Farrell. It's not that I don't appreciate all you've done for me, it's just that – well, I left in such a hurry, so unexpectedly, and I'm feeling perfectly well again, and anxious to – to get back, that's all.'

Her eyes pleaded for understanding.

'Don't take on too much too soon, then, Madeleine,' he advised her seriously. 'Young bones mend readily, I know, and there's no reason to believe yours will be different, but your whole system has had a shake-up, obviously. You look on the point of collapse, if you want the blunt truth – far worse than you did at the time!'

Maddie smiled. It was a wan effort, quite unlike the lovely transforming smile that Skeet so loved.

'I'm all right, truly. I promise I won't do too much.'

I won't do *anything*, in fact, she thought grimly – except our packing! There was no point now in going on with the painting or the garden, or even those driving lessons!

When she got back to Yattabilla, the first thing Maddie did was to clean all the paintbrushes and put away the paint and ladder. Her right arm was back to normal, and she found herself removing the left one from its sling and using it cautiously, without causing her collarbone any discomfort.

She had decided that she would say nothing to Skeet until he came home for the week-end. (Funny how she had got to thinking of Yattabilla as 'home', she thought, with bitter irony, just when they were going to have to leave it.) She intended to be absolutely ready to leave when Friday came, and they would catch the day train on Saturday morning. That way, Skeet wouldn't even have long in which to think about it. The break would be made, cleanly and swiftly – and permanently!

Maddie knew that she could count on Tom Simson to help her to get to the station. He had been a kind and understanding friend, and since he was young and eager to please – without that domineering, autocratic streak that Steve had, for instance – it would be easy enough to work him round to co-operating with her plans. If he could not come for them himself, Maddie would ask him to hire a car on her behalf. She had enough money to pay for that and their second-class fares to Sydney, and a little left, over and beyond, for their first week or so in the city.

She was going to miss Tom, and Noonday, she realized with a sad little pang. Tom had been like an elder brother to her. Straight away she had felt for him the kinship of youth. He was fun to be with when she went to Noonday, and the town itself had been so peaceful and friendly, too.

The week was spent mending and washing her own and Skeet's few belongings. She polished their shoes, ironed shorts and shirts, and packed everything neatly into the two shabby cases and the canvas hold-all.

On Friday she switched off the kerosene refrigerator and removed the fuel tray, emptied the lamps and trimmed the wicks. Looking about her, she could not help contrasting the shining cleanliness everywhere with the discouraging filth on her arrival. At least she had struck a blow for poor old Yattabilla, she thought wryly. It had been her father's house, after all – the place where she herself had been born – and it was the richer, rather than the poorer, for her short stay in it. She felt she had made a positive contribution, however slight, to its preservation. From now on, it would be for Steve to take over. Perhaps he would even depute Kareena to arrange for something to be done with it, although Maddie could not imagine the future mistress of Bibbi bothering herself with such an unglamorous assignment!

After she had done all the last-minute chores in the house, Maddie rang Tom.

She was fortunate to get him at the office. She knew that with Tom alone she could cope, but not with the added complication of maternal distress and disapproval that Mrs. Simson would be sure to voice.

Even Tom himself was difficult. It took all Maddie's not inconsiderable persuasive powers to make him even think of doing what she wanted, and she found herself actually begging desperately, with tears in her voice, before he finally and reluctantly conceded.

Maddie put down the receiver. She felt limp with the

effort. Thank heaven she only had to go through it all once! Soon she and Skeet would be away from here, and then she would have to set about pulling herself together, and making some sort of new life for them both.

She went and had a bath, then washed her hair, awkwardly, because doing so necessitated holding her arm at a rather awkward angle. It took a long time, but in the end she was satisfied that the golden strands squeaked with cleanliness. She brushed it out into a polished curtain, prepared herself a quick snack for lunch, and then sat down and wrote a letter to Robert.

Maddie had known all week that she was going to have to write that letter, because she knew, finally and irrevocably, that she could never marry Robert – not when her heart was already given to Steve.

She could not compare the two men, even hypothetically, as prospective husbands. She trusted Robert, respected him and liked him, but she did not love him – and no marriage at all was better than one without love.

She could never give herself to Robert's arms while, in her heart, she longed for the strong, muscular ones of Steve Darley about her. She could never again put her lips to Robert's without remembering the butterfly brush of Steve's firm cool ones against her damaged brow. In her heart of hearts, Maddie knew that she could never love again. Steve's place there was for always – however futile and hopeless.

Maddie found Robert's a difficult letter to write. She intended to post it in Noonday in the morning, because she did not mean to get in touch with him again in Sydney – or not for a long, long time. He was so kind, so responsible, that he would feel the need to take care of them and keep an eye on them. He might even use their situation as a pressure point for an early marriage, and Maddie did not wish to burden him with the knowledge that she and Skeet were once more on their own. She felt that would be unfair to Robert, and if he really did imagine himself to be in love with her, it would be kinder to keep right out of his way. Maddie was sure that he would soon forget her, and find some other more rewarding romance, if she did that.

She simply explained that she could never marry him, but that she valued his continued friendship, and left it at that. She sealed the envelope, licked a stamp and put it on the corner, and then went to her bedroom and placed the letter carefully in her handbag, so that she would not forget to post it in the morning.

Out of her bedroom window Maddie caught sight of a dust-cloud. It was away along the track, about the place where the wrecked Buick had been. It certainly could not be the Buick, because that vehicle was roadworthy no longer, alas! — and in any case, Steve had had Lal tow it into one of the sheds. Neither could it be the school bus, which was not due for another hour or more.

Maddie watched the dust-cloud in a fascinated way as it moved along fast, nearer and nearer to the Yattabilla homestead. When it was quite close, she drew in her breath sharply, and her knees became so weak and wobbly that she had to clutch the window-sill to support herself.

It was Steve's car, the big Chevrolet. He was alone.

Maddie saw him get out, slam the door behind him with unnecessary force, and come striding quickly up the path. Then she heard his elastic-sided stockman's boots clattering over the verandah. The gauze door banged.

'Madeleine?' He sounded breathless.

Maddie smoothed her newly-dried, shining hair with fingers that trembled, and went into the hall to meet him. They faced each other across the bare stretch of pine flooring.

Steve's face was grim, the grooves at the sides of his mouth deep and taut, pulling his lips into a compressed, forbidding line. His grey eyes were dark, smouldering with anger.

'What's this ridiculous nonsense I hear from Tom Simson, about you leaving Yattabilla?' he asked, without further hesitation.

Maddie stiffened. 'It isn't nonsense at all.' She did her best to sound cool. 'In any case, it was between Tom and me. He had no right to tell you.'

'He had every right,' Steve contradicted tersely. 'For once the young ass did the right thing where you're concerned. He was worried and he got in touch with me.'

'It has absolutely nothing to do with you,' she protested.

'Oh, yes, it has! It has plenty to do with me! I'm your father's trustee, which young Simson fortunately seems to know. He also knows that if you go away, you forfeit your inheritance. I suppose you told him the legal angle at some point, and luckily he took it in.'

'Luck doesn't enter into it either way.' Maddie steeled herself into calmness. Now, if ever, she had to test her powers as an actress. 'I realize that by leaving I shall forfeit my right to Yattabilla, and it doesn't worry me in the least. What's more, it's nobody's business but my own.'

Steve's jaw hardened.

'You mean you're *serious*?'

Maddie nodded. 'Perfectly serious. I'm leaving tomorrow, by the day train – with Skeet, of course.'

Steve's probing glance became incredulous. The incredulity was swiftly banished by suspicion. His eyes got narrow, more keenly penetrating than ever.

'Madeleine, why?' A few strides brought him right to her side. 'Why the sudden change? Heavens, it's not more than a few weeks since you were digging in your toes, cursing me to hell, and telling me you'd see the thing through at all costs. What's happened to knock the stuffing out of you?' His voice deepened in concern. 'It's that blasted accident, Madeleine. You haven't given yourself a chance to get over it properly. Don't do anything hasty while you're still feeling under the weather. Come back to Bibbi for a little while, and you'll see things differently. I knew you weren't fit, and I shouldn't have allowed you to persuade me that you were. A week or two more, and you'll have got your fighting spirit back – it's one of the things I admire about you, that spunk! I'll fix it with old Opal.'

Maddie swallowed a lump in her throat. When Steve was as near as this, looking down at her with almost tender persuasion, she found it difficult to be strong. But she *must*!

'No, Steve.' She shook her head. 'My mind is quite made up.'

He was silent for a moment.

'There has to be a reason,' he said at length. 'Why are you doing this, Madeleine? What's changed your mind for you?'

Maddie blinked, stared woodenly at the middle button of his khaki shirt which was on a level with her own eyes. Yes, Steve was right. There had to be a reason. She had to *find* a reason. Any reason at all would do, so long as it wasn't the right one!

She blinked again, muttered a silent prayer for inspiration, and as if in answer to her prayer, inspiration came.

'Robert has asked me to marry him.'

Steve's eyes locked with hers. He stood incredibly still.

'Is that true?'

'Absolutely.' It wasn't a lie, anyway, she told herself a little desperately. Robert *had* asked her to marry him. She was only *implying* that she had accepted, after all.

'Yes, that figures.' Steve was speaking almost to himself. 'You did look pretty shaken when you had to leave him that day. I wonder why I didn't think of that!'

'One doesn't like to make things too obvious, does one?' suggested Maddie demurely. 'I mean, one doesn't like to wear one's heart on one's sleeve.'

What an actress she was turning out to be! She had had no idea that she would be capable of bringing so much conviction to her role!

'No, that's right.' Steve's voice was oddly strained. He walked abruptly to the window, and stood there looking out.

In profile his stern features were expressionless and still, save for a small muscle that jerked somewhere near his jaw. When he turned to her again the stormy look had left his eyes. They were composed, almost bleak, and his face beneath its deep tan had the alabaster pallor of the Sphinx itself.

'Very well, Madeleine, I accept your explanation.' A pause. 'I can only hope that you'll be very happy.'

'You, too, Steve,' she whispered, with tears in her eyes.

You and Kareena, she wanted to say. I hope you and Kareena will be happy, too, Steve, because I couldn't bear it if you weren't happy, even if it has to be with her.

'I'll leave it to you to tell Mr. Opal,' she said. 'From now on, it will be for the two of you to arrange. Good-bye, Steve.'

She put out her hand formally, felt it taken in a firm grasp. She wanted to cling to that hard brown hand, to beg him to feel a little bit for her what she was feeling for him just now. But she couldn't, of course – and anyway, what was the use? She was no more to him than a tiresome and inconvenient responsibility, of whom he would soon be rid, and then he could go right ahead and marry his Kareena.

'I'll say good-bye to Skeet for you. I think it would be better if he didn't see you again.'

The ghost of a smile twisted Steve's set mouth.

'Do that, Madeleine. For once I agree with you about what's best for Skeet, it seems.'

Those were the last words he said to Maddie. He didn't look back when he reached the car, not even to wave farewell. Maddie was watching, hoping that he might, but he started the engine and left without a backward glance, even though she stood at the fence until his car was right out of sight.

Telling Skeet proved almost worse than telling Steve. At first he could only blink disbelievingly, and then, as he saw that Maddie really meant every word she said, the freckles began to stand out as his face lost colour.

'But why do we have to go, Maddie? Why? I like it here, and I thought we had to stay for a year. I don't *want* to go, Maddie!'

She sighed, squaring her thin shoulders.

'We have to go, Skeet, for reasons that you're too young to understand. Some day, when you're grown up, I'll tell you all about them, and then you'll see that it was the only thing. I promise you there's no other way. You'll just have to trust me to look after us both, darling. It won't be so bad. I thought you quite liked Sydney?'

He stared at her mutinously.

'I like Noonday best. I like the school there, too. It's the best fun I've ever had.' His small face brightened as a thought struck him. 'Maddie, couldn't we stop in Noonday if we have to leave here? I could stay at school, then, and you could get a job. You like Noonday, too. You *love* it, same as me, I know you do! Gee, that'd be great!'

Her heart turned with anguish, because she knew she was going to have to drive that eagerness right out of Skeet's wiry little frame. Noonday? And see Kareena and Steve even more often than she would here at Yattabilla? Impossible!

'No, Skeet, I'm sorry, it's out of the question. We have to go *right* away. But I'll make it up to you, pet. We'll have good times down there in the city, once we get settled somewhere. You'll see!'

Skeet shook his head. Without replying, he got up and left the room, and a few minutes later Maddie saw his disconsolate form wandering aimlessly outside, kicking a pebble in front of him with the toe of his new brown sandal. Later still, she spotted him walking with more purpose towards the fowlyard.

When she went to make the tea, her mind was still on her own problems, and the unpleasant things she yet had to do — like trying to explain to Tom, for instance, when he took them to Noonday in the morning. She was totally unprepared, therefore, for the almost hysterical sound of sobbing which reached her ears as she was pouring boiling water into the teapot.

Maddie put down the kettle quickly, and rushed outside. Skeet was leaning up against the verandah post, crying as if his heart would break.

She knelt down beside him and drew him into her arms, feeling his small body, wracked with distress, shivering against her.

'Skeet darling, what is it?' She stroked the ginger spikes of hair, smoothing them down with a soothing touch. 'It won't be as bad as all that, Skeet, truly it won't. I wouldn't do it if I didn't have to, but I'll make it up to you. You wait and see. We've always managed to have fun, haven't we, even when things were at their worst?'

'It isn't that.' The words were strangled.

'What then?'

'It's Etta.'

'Etta?'

He nodded miserably, trying to control himself.

'What about Etta, Skeet? She's fine. I've been looking after her for you, the same as always. She was all right this morning.'

'*She's* all right, but – Maddie–' his voice quavered all over again '—she's left her nest, Maddie, an' she's broken all the eggs. I *saw* her! It wasn't that I was disturbing her or anything, honestly, I promise. She just suddenly got up as if she was terrible angry, and she scratched about as if she'd gone mad an' she broke every one.' He sobbed afresh. 'There's no chicks in them, Maddie. We're not going to get chicks after all. They're just a lot of rotten old eggs! Rotten! *Rotten!*'

He kicked fiercely at the verandah post, and a bit of timber that the white ants had attacked went flying off into the weeds where the garden had once been.

It only needed this! Maddie told herself, distraught for her little brother. It only needed this!

'They weren't the right sort of eggs, Skeet,' she comforted

him sadly. 'They couldn't have been, could they? Nothing's right for us here, darling. We thought it was going to be, but *nothing's* right! Things will be different when we go. We'll put it all behind us. We'll forget all about those rotten old eggs and – and – everything.' She took his hand. 'Come on in. I've made the tea. Scones, too.'

Skeet ran his sleeve over his tear-stained face and came.

In the morning, Maddie laid out his clean things for him to put on for the train, and dressed in her emerald shift. She knew she would get hot and sticky on the journey, and she must keep her cotton two-piece with the white collar to wear in Sydney when she was job-hunting next week. It was essential to appear neat and well-groomed when you were a rather ordinary sort of shorthand-typist, unable to boast the devastating speeds of efficiency which some of her colleagues at the business college had achieved!

She found herself hampered scarcely at all by the sling now. In fact, she was using her arm quite normally, and only bothered to tuck it into the supporting fold of cloth when there was nothing else she was wanting to do with it. She would see a doctor about a final clearance when she had found somewhere for herself and Skeet to stay. That was the first priority.

When she and Skeet had breakfasted, she carried the suit-cases and canvas bag on to the verandah, locked the doors, and took the keys down to Mrs. Lawrence – not that there was a likelihood of anyone using the house, but it seemed an appropriate and responsible gesture.

Mrs. Lawrence looked her over curiously when she handed in the keys.

'I ain't surprised at you clearin' out so quick. Some might be, but *I* ain't. I said you was like your ma all along,' she said, nasal and unfriendly as ever.

'Please tell Lal that we don't need any more meat, Mrs. Lawrence,' Maddie returned evenly. 'And I'd be grateful if you'll keep an eye on the hens, too.'

'It won't matter to you, will it? You'll be gone, see. And

anyway, it's Mr. Darley that gives me my orders. If Mr. Darley tells me to look after the poultry, I'll look after it.'

Maddie felt there was nothing to be gained by a response. She turned and walked back to the house, and not long after that, Tom came to collect them.

It was easy enough to discourage a post-mortem of her decision with Tom. She hated herself as she did it, but she simply raised her eyebrows, glanced meaningly in Skeet's direction, and whispered, 'Not *now*, Tom. Don't say anything in front of *him*, please.'

Maddie knew she was safe in saying that, because Skeet would be with her all the time from now until the moment when they boarded the train at Noonday station.

Skeet jumped out eagerly when the first gate came. Maddie felt her heart contract when she remembered who had taught him how to open it and all the others, on that very first trip out to Yattabilla. Steve's voice echoed in her ears, patient, amused, and firm in alternating degrees. He had always been kind to Skeet, she had to admit that – kind, almost fatherly – even though he had approached her with that astringent cynicism which had the effect of making her brace up inwardly, determined to fight her own battles.

Maddie could have done with some bracing-up right now. There was not much fight left in her! She was feeling something of a failure, and Tom's worried face and slightly resentful silence served only to add to her sense of guilt and hopelessness.

The plains, today, were at their most beautiful, with that oddly stark, contradictory splendour that dry, sun-drenched country sometimes has. Away to their right, the ridge reared up, a freak of nature, majestic in a purple haze of distance against the pale, cloudless sky. Maddie took her last long look at that ridge, tried to forget that Bibbi lay on its western flank.

'Good-bye, old monster,' she murmured under her breath, but the monster slumbered on, impervious to her farewell just as he had been oblivious to the mortal comings and goings about him ever since prehistory.

When they arrived in Noonday, Tom carried their bags on to the platform, and Maddie took Skeet to the news agency to buy some reading material, a bottle of lemonade and some sweets. She also bought a bag of apples, and several oranges, recalling her brother's biliousness on the journey out. Steve had been right about that, too. It was true that she had indulged Skeet freely with all sorts of sickly rubbish to which he had pointed on the confectioner's counter at Sydney. This time, she was firm!

On the way back to the platform, she posted her letter to Robert. It would have the Noonday postmark on it, so that he would never need to know that she was at Yattabilla no longer. She would not contact him again until she had achieved a measure of security and independence for herself and Skeet in Sydney. At the present moment she felt too vulnerable to trust herself, and realized that, out of sheer weak relief at the thought of a masculine arm to lean on, marriage to Robert could become a very real temptation. It would also be a mistake, and one which she intended to avoid, at whatever cost to herself just now.

There were few enough travellers on the train this morning. It was a small train, too.

'It doesn't take on more carriages until it reaches the big junction in the wheat belt,' Tom explained. 'That's where most of the Sydney-bound passengers get on. If they live as far out as this, they often use planes, you see, Maddie.'

When the whistle blew, Maddie received Tom's shy, rather fumbled kiss in silence. What, indeed, could she say that would not sound hopelessly inadequate after his goodness to her? As the train moved slowly away from the platform, her final glimpse was of him standing there, in his white, open-necked shirt, holding his wide felt hat in his hand, and looking after them with a sort of puzzled, fond bewilderment.

Maddie could not blame him. She still felt a certain bewilderment herself!

CHAPTER ELEVEN

MADDIE decided that she must put that first awful two weeks back in Sydney right out of her mind.

It did not do to dwell on the past, even the very recent past, she told herself firmly, remembering all the miles she had walked searching for the type of accommodation that she could afford, recalling all those fruitless interviews with every employment agency she could find in the telephone directory.

The trouble arose over the question of hours. She had hoped for permanent work for a certain period each day, so that she could be at home to welcome Skeet when he came in from school. It was depressing enough for him to have to return to the dingy room which they were occupying, without finding that room empty.

The landlady did not care for children. In fact, when Maddie had confessed to possessing a small brother, she had almost snatched the lease-form right out of her prospective tenant's hand!

'I don't hold with kids,' she had said censoriously, as if she herself had plunged straight from the cradle into adulthood, escaping that tiresome juvenile state altogether. 'They don't care a fig for other folk's property, especially boys, I've always found. Ten's about the worst age of the lot, if you ask me! I don't really think I can take you, after all. If I'd known about *him* at the start, I wouldn't even have considered it.'

Maddie had had to plead. She was footsore, pale, and desperate. Maybe her own appearance had something to do with the landlady's final capitulation. The result was that Maddie felt it a matter of necessity to keep Skeet under constant surveillance. If she was not there when he returned from the school each day, she quailed to think what pranks he might get up to in her absence. For the same reason, she did not dare to take on supplementary employment in the evenings. She had been able to do that in London only because of the landlady's motherly co-operation in keeping an eye on Skeet for her.

Because she could not work after three o'clock, and not at all on Saturdays, Maddie's salary was pruned accordingly. She could not argue with the fairness of that, but it meant that she was earning barely enough to pay for the room and to keep herself and Skeet in any sort of comfort. She went without even the tiniest luxury for herself, and sometimes without necessities as well, giving Skeet the biggest helpings of food when it came to meal-times, because he still had a lot of growing to do, and mending her clothes as they became threadbare. Grimly she realized that she could afford no replacements at present. Nostalgically she found herself remembering those vast piles of butchered meat which Lal used to bring up to the homestead twice a week, and the Yattabilla account which Steve had urged her to use without hesitation if she should need anything. These were changed days now!

Summer turned to autumn, and the weather changed to cold, windy days and blustery nights when a thin mist of rain blinded the small top-floor window of their shared bed-sitter.

Maddie got soaked one day returning from work, and although she changed her clothes immediately, she succumbed a few days afterwards to a bad bout of 'flu. The doctor, grudgingly summoned by her landlady, insisted on a whole week in bed, and another of convalescence.

Maddie wrote a postcard to her employer, apologizing for the inconvenience her absence would doubtless cause, and asked Skeet to post it. When she received no reply, she began to fret. Perhaps no news was good news, but it could also imply her pending dismissal, and in her present physical state she wondered how she could possibly go through the wearisome procedure of finding employment all over again.

'You did post the card, didn't you, Skeet?' She croaked the question huskily from her bed.

'Yes, Maddie, honest I did. I put it in the post-box at the corner.'

She passed her hand over her aching brow.

'Maybe they just haven't acknowledged it. Or maybe they're going to fire me. I won't know till I go back. Anyway,' she smiled into her little brother's suddenly anxious face, 'I don't like it much there, Skeet. It's not much of a job. I'll *easily* get something better!'

He appeared reassured, to her own relief. She must not let Skeet see how worried she was! He had been so sweet and helpful while she was in bed, and even before that, too. A new closeness had sprung up between them, as if both realized how completely interdependent they were upon each other for comfort and what little happiness they could find in this new, rather grim, phase of their lives. She would not mention it again!

By the middle of the second week, Maddie realized that the doctor had been right to insist on an additional period of convalescence. She was not picking up as quickly as she had hoped. Certainly her limbs no longer ached with those influenzal pains, and her sore throat was quite better, too, but she felt curiously languid.

She was glad to remain in bed in the mornings, and in the afternoons she would wander listlessly about the room in her dressing-gown, knowing that she would have felt warmer under the blankets, but appreciating the necessity of getting her strength back with the help of some exercise. The coins she put in the slot for the gas fire didn't seem to make it hot for very long, and she had worked out a daily ration of money for that purpose – more than she could afford, really, but it barely served to take the chill dampness out of the air.

She was doing just that – wandering about the room, tidying up Skeet's colouring books and crayons which were still where he had left them before school this morning, flicking a duster half-heartedly over the few pieces of furniture – when there was a knock at the door.

Maddie hesitated. It was too early for Skeet, so it must be the landlady. As always when she had a visit from the landlady, she felt a small knot of anxiety and apprehension tightening her stomach muscles. Some day soon she was bound to be given notice to leave, and maybe that day had arrived! Skeet had been in a boisterous mood last night, restless because the weather had stopped all outdoor games in the school playground, bored because Maddie could not even take him out for a walk in the rain. He had made more noise than he intended, and the landlady had complained.

She went to the door and opened it, and when she saw who was there, she froze where she stood, wide-eyed, clutching the folds of her shabby dressing-gown closer.

'Madeleine?' It was half question, half statement. 'Aren't you going to invite me in?'

'Steve.' She could hardly breathe his name. 'Why have you come?' she managed to ask huskily.

Steve's white teeth flashed in his wet, brown face, but his eyes were oddly serious and the banter in his voice did not quite ring true.

'Looking for Madeleine Janet Masterton, that's why I'm here.' A mock sigh. 'I seem to have spent a good deal of time looking for Madeleine Janet Masterton, do you know that, Madeleine? First in London, and now in Sydney. The trouble is – as soon as I find her, she sort of slips away.'

Maddie continued to stare. She was swaying on her feet.

Steve, characteristically, did not wait for that invitation he had suggested, since it did not appear to be forthcoming anyway. He took her firmly by the hand, propelled her inside, and shut the door behind him. He was wearing a grey city suit, but not the one he had worn the first time, all those months ago. This one was equally well cut, but of a heavier weight. Maddie could see that his broad shoulders were dark with rain, and it glistened on his lean, tanned cheeks as he stood there just inside the door, looking down at her strangely.

The bantering tone wasn't there any more when he spoke again.

'Come clean, Madeleine.' He gave her a little shake. 'Why did you do it? Why did you run out on me? And don't try any more of your nasty little inventions on me, either! You won't get away with it a second time, I'm warning you – especially not here!' He made a gesture of distaste which somehow encompassed the whole of the shabby set-up that surrounded them, his eyes taking in his environs in a single disparaging sweep before they came to rest on her once more. 'You're shivering. I forgot you'd been ill. We can talk just as well sitting down. Get into that chair.'

She sank into it in wordless obedience.

'You haven't even a fire!' he condemned tersely, kneeling down in front of the gas affair in the hearth. 'How does this damn thing work?'

'With coins.' Maddie found her voice. 'B-but I've run out of change,' she lied weakly.

There was a muttered oath from the man squatting at the fireplace. He stood up, sorted through a handful of money from his trousers pocket for the appropriate coins, jabbed them into the slot, and turned the switch.

'You could do with a good spanking,' he told her repressively, as he took the chair opposite her own, 'And if you hadn't just had 'flu, that's what you'd get, make no mistake about that!'

One part of her brain registered the cold, suppressed fury in the way he spoke those words, while another bewildered part grappled with the puzzle of just how he could possibly know she'd had 'flu.

Was the man psychic, or something? He certainly was behaving very oddly! He looked, in fact, not only capable of beating her as he had threatened, but even of boring right into her mind to see what she was thinking if his psychic powers should fail him! Steve Darley was sitting there, big and menacing and much too large for that flimsy wicker chair, looking as if he might be capable of anything!

'Well, Madeleine?' he suggested in a carefully controlled voice. 'Let's have your story – and no more flights into the realms of fancy this time. I won't fall for it twice!'

Maddie swallowed on a peculiar constriction in her throat. She couldn't think of a single thing to say, just then.

'H-how did you find out where I was?' she asked, after a painful interval spent groping wildly for some safe topic.

A little grimly, Steve reached into the inner pocket of his jacket.

'I had a letter,' he informed her, taking out an envelope. 'From Skeet.'

'From *Skeet*?' Maddie sat bolt upright in surprise.

'From Skeet. Like to hear it?'

Without waiting for her assent, he withdrew the folded sheet and read.

'Dear Steve, I hope you are well.' He paused. 'It's dated just three days ago, by the way, and the address is your present one.'

'Go on,' she whispered. This was dreadful!

'I hope you are well. I am writing to you in class, because we are learning how, and the teacher says if we write a letter real good we can post it. Her name is Miss Sparrow and she has got a stamp and we can even lick it ourselves and put it on so as we will know for another time. Your address is the only one I know except for Maddie, and it would be silly to write to her when we live in the same room, anyway, so I hope you don't mind. Maddie has had 'flu and she was awful sick but the landlady brung drinks twice and I got tea. I got boiled eggs two nights and another time I got beans. We have got a stove and you use matches to light it. Maddie might lose her job but she doesn't care because she says it isn't very nice anyway.'

A small, involuntary sound from Maddie made him look up.

174

'Do you want me to go on?' he asked in level tones.

She nodded. 'You may as well finish,' she agreed lamely.

'I was sorry I couldn't say good-bye when we left Yatta-billa because I would have told you that Etta's eggs was rotten, the whole lot, and there was no chicks inside after all, so we got nothing. Maddie said there was nothing for us there anyhow, but I reckon there could have been chicks only there wasn't. She said they weren't the right sort of eggs. I hardly cried at all. With lots of love from Skeet.'

In silence he folded the page carefully, put it back into its envelope and returned it to his pocket.

'Well?'

Maddie stared at the floor, twisting her hands together nervously. She wished she could think of something to say, but there seemed to be a temporary paralysis of her mental processes.

'Why did you do it, Madeleine?' Steve's voice was deep, insistent.

She shook her head, shrugged helplessly.

'I don't know.' It sounded weak.

Steve must have thought it sounded weak, too, because he got up out of the chair, walked over and put his hands on her restless fingers. He drew her purposefully to her feet to face him.

'Of course you know,' he contradicted her gently. 'There had to be a reason, didn't there, Maddie?'

He used the contraction of her name without seeming aware of it. His eyes were searching hers, but there was a tenderness softening their grey depths, and his mouth was kind. It was just above her own.

Maddie stared at that mouth, mesmerized.

'There had to be a reason, hadn't there?' His lips murmured the words, against her ear. 'Will you give me the right reason this time, Maddie? The honest one?'

Maddie felt his hands relinquish their grasp on her fingers and move to her back. Then she felt them drawing her towards him until she was right up against him, so that her eyes were on a level with the middle shirt button of his neat, pin-striped shirt. Steve's square-tipped brown fingers tilted her chin upwards, so that she had to look at him.

'Maybe this will help to give you a clue,' he whispered huskily. Maddie watched his lips curve, in the merest hint of a smile, and then they came down gently on to hers.

Steve's kiss was restrained at first, and then Maddie felt his arms crushing her to him as passion took over. He was kissing her now with a swift mastery and possessiveness that brought such a heavenly weakness to her limbs that she could only cling to him. And then she was returning his kiss, with all the love she had bottled up secretly for so long.

Presently he straightened, put her away from him and watched her. There was a curious expression on his face, a mixture of triumph and relief.

'So two and two appear to make four after all,' he murmured obliquely, in an oddly shaken voice. He took her shoulders and gave her a tiny, reproving shake that was somehow an endearment as well. 'Now we know the truth, don't we? We know the reason, don't we, darling?' he persisted, as she continued to feast her eyes on him in wonder.

'Yes, Steve,' she whispered.

'You didn't intend to marry Robert when you went away, did you?'

'No, Steve.'

'You just said that to fob me off. You didn't intend to marry *anyone*.'

'No, Steve.'

'You were running away, weren't you, Maddie?'

'Yes.'

'Who were you running away from, Maddie?' he asked, with laughter in his voice. 'From me?'

'I suppose it must have been. I don't know.' She dropped her eyes. She was shy of this new, unfamiliar Steve.

He gave a deep chuckle.

'Yes, you do. We both know now, don't we? You ran away because you'd found out that you didn't hate me any more. You'd fallen in love and you wanted to escape, because you didn't know, you silly little darling spitfire, that I'd fallen in love with you, too.'

'How *could* I know? How could I guess?' she defended herself, still in a state of dreamy unreality at the turn her life had taken in this past half-hour.

Steve's eyes devoured her.

'No, Maddie, I'm sorry.' He was sober all at once. 'You couldn't have guessed, little one – not even if you'd had far more experience of such things than I can tell you've had – because I didn't intend that you should know. I loved you from the moment I set eyes on you in old Opal's office – that wonderful hair and creamy skin, your brave little independent spirit that defied me from the start – what a combination! I knew right then and there that one day I meant to have you, but at that stage you hated me. Oh, yes, you did!' He dropped a kiss on the point of her chin. 'Remember what you said the day we said good-bye at Yattabilla, Maddie – about not wearing one's heart on one's sleeve?'

'Yes, Steve, I remember every word we said that day.'

'Well, by God, that shaft went home, because that's precisely how it was with me. I couldn't wear my heart on my sleeve. If I had, I'd have scared you off. You'd have thought I was simply after Yattabilla, and you wouldn't have believed me anyway.'

He passed a hand over his eyes. Only then did Maddie notice how pale he was, and there was an unfamiliar tremor in the usually capable fingers that passed themselves across his forehead as if trying to erase some painful memory. Just for a moment, he was the old, grim Steve, not the tender, loving one who had been kissing her a short while ago.

'I thought I had a year, you see, Maddie. I thought I had a whole year, but dear heaven, how wrong can a man be? I meant to wait until Yattabilla became yours, and then, I thought, I'd take it slowly from there. At first I wanted you to leave that wretched homestead — it was torture thinking of you battling away there on your own, and I really did think you might stand a chance of getting the place some other way. And then I realized that if you tried it and failed, I'd have lost your trust for ever. It was an unenviable choice, but in the end I reckoned you'd be better to stay and see the thing through, and the only way I could help you to do it was by rather brutal means, I admit — jibing at you when I felt you might be losing your nerve, making you angry when your courage faltered, and so forth. It was hell! Anyway, I got to planning what I'd do once the year was up. I'd give you time — lots of time — so that gradually you would learn to trust me. Once you trusted me I knew I'd have the battle half won, and that I could make you love me the way I loved you.'

'Oh, Steve!' There were tears in Maddie's eyes — tears of love and joy and incredible wonder that Steve could be saying these things to her, when all the time she had thought he and Kareena— 'I didn't know.'

'Of course you didn't,' he took her hand, sat down in the upholstered chair which Maddie herself had occupied, and pulled her on to his knee. From the haven of his arms she went on listening. 'I nearly gave myself away, just once, and it was only when I got Skeet's note and started thinking things out that I realized things just might have been different if I had revealed my feelings after all.'

Maddie nodded.

'When I had the accident?'

'You knew?'

'I thought I was dreaming. You called me darling! Oh, Steve, did you really call me that? I didn't dream it, after all?'

'I really did.' He held her close. 'I was demented with worry. By the time I had searched and couldn't find you, I was nearly out of my mind. I hardly knew what I was saying — but I also knew what I *mustn't* say! It just slipped out somehow.' He grinned, self-mocking. 'I didn't think you'd heard.'

'I *think* you said it twice.'

'Probably I did. I was having a pretty tough time keeping my feelings under control at all.' A pause. 'And then you went away. You told me you were going to marry Robert, and suddenly there was not a future that included me at all. There was no reason for planning what I'd do in a year, because you'd gone away.' He passed a hand over his eyes in a replica of that former painful gesture, unaware that he did so. 'They were unpleasant weeks, Maddie, those ones after you left. I wondered how the hell I could go on living! I put Kareena on a plane, and then I got to grips with Opal, about the property. I've had it transferred from my name to Skeet's, by the way. It's in trust for him, and he'll come into it when he's of age.'

'Oh, *Steve*!'

'Well, darling, he is Gerald's son. He had a greater moral claim than anyone else to it, and I must say I felt a little better once I'd done that. It takes a while for these transfers to be properly drawn up, of course, but the solicitors would have tried to contact you as Robert's wife in order to let you know, and we'd have found out then that you had not married him at all! I'd have been out of my mind, Madeleine,' – he regarded her reprovingly – 'because *none* of us would have had any idea where to find you! I'd have tracked you down somehow, be sure of that, little one – you wouldn't have escaped me for long, but thank the lord Skeet wrote me when he did! He saved me one hell of a frantic search. He's a great little cobber, is Skeet.'

His arms tightened, and they kissed again. This time Steve did it with gentleness and understanding, in a way that told her she need not worry any more. They trusted each other at last. They had *found* each other.

'I can hardly believe it, Maddie – that your feelings have changed to this extent. It was either very sudden, or you've been a damn good actress for a very long time. Which?'

'It happened a long while ago,' Maddie replied dreamily.

'I realize that now. I thought I hated you, because I didn't know what the symptoms meant, that's all. I've never been in love before – not properly, not this way, and I can see now that I was awfully ignorant.' She touched his tanned cheek with one finger, ran it down the groove beside his mouth. 'I think I did hate you at first, Steve. Well, maybe hate's too strong a word. It was dislike, because you made me feel all shaken and peculiar inside, and I didn't know why. You disturbed me, and I resented it. I only really hated you just once, and that was when I found out that you'd conspired with Mrs. Lawrence to scare me off.'

'When I – *what*?' Steve was startled.

'When I heard her telling you she had left the house just like you said – out the kitchen window. You rode over on your horse, remember, and we quarrelled about Skeet's schooling, and you met her as you were leaving, near the garden fence, and I heard.'

He sighed exaggeratedly.

'Maddie, my girl, try to make a little sense, will you, darling? I'm afraid I simply can't see why my speaking to Mrs. Lawrence should make you hate me!'

She flushed.

'You do *remember* speaking to her?'

'Certainly I do. I asked her if she had left everything in the house the way I had said, and she replied that she had. What harm is there in that, you little goose?' His tone was teasing.

Maddie pulled herself away from him indignantly.

'Steve Darley, I'm afraid I don't think it was funny! I didn't then, and I don't now.' Her eyes glittered at the memory. 'Steve, how *could* you! All those cobwebs and the dirt and grease, and the mice in the mattresses, and all those dead flies in the windows – *hundreds* of them, even if they *were* dead! – and anyway, those big fat spiders weren't! *They* were alive, and I had to shut my eyes when I—'

'Hey, steady on.' He had stopped smiling. His eyes got narrow, and the warmth drained away, leaving them cold, like slits of ice. 'Just what are you trying to get across?'

Maddie's eyes locked with his, hers still defiant, his increasingly thoughtful. He put her firmly off his knee and stood up, tall and very forbidding, with his back to the flickering gaslight.

'I admit I checked with Mrs. Lawrence that day to see that she had left things as I said,' Steve told her carefully, 'and what I had told her was this. I told her to clean up that hell-hole of a homestead, to scour it from top to bottom, with carbolic if need be, to see that the kitchen was spruce and the rooms shipshape and the beds made up, and to make sure that—'

Maddie's giggle halted him. It only began as a tiny one, but it somehow took possession of her until she shook with uncontrollable, almost hysterical mirth.

'Maddie, stop it, for heaven's sake!' barked Steve. 'It's I who am not amused now! Listen to me, Madeleine' — he took her by the shoulders, 'are you trying to tell me that that house *wasn't* like I ordered? Are you saying that—?' He could only shake his head helplessly. Words appeared to have failed him.

'I wish you'd seen it!' Maddie wiped tears of laughter from the corners of her eyes. 'The kapok was strewn all over the floor, and the mice, or rats, or whatever they were, had—'

'You needn't go over it all again, Maddie. I get the general idea.' He began to stride restlessly about the tiny room, grim-faced. 'My God, I'll have her hide when I get back! The scheming witch! I'll get to the bottom of it, and find out what goes on in that woman's mind. I'll have the truth, and before heaven, she's going to regret it!' he muttered savagely.

'Darling.' Maddie ran to him and put her hand on his sleeve. 'It doesn't matter now, Steve, can't you see? It doesn't matter any more, now that I know *you* weren't involved. She can't hurt us now, even if she tried. She was never nice to me, the whole time I was there. She looked at me with real hatred the very first morning, and told me I wouldn't stay long. She said I was like my mother.'

'Did she, by Jove! I'm beginning to wonder just how much she had to do with *that* breaking up, now I think about it. She's nothing much better than a malicious mischief-maker! Obviously she's got a grudge against her own sex. There *are* people like that, and the fact that butter wouldn't ever melt in her mouth with either myself or Gerald bears it out! Anyway, Maddie, you can forget about her. You won't need to see her again. Lal's one of the best station-hands there is, but he'll be retired by the time Skeet takes on the running of the place, and Mrs. Lawrence will be out of the way.'

Steve pulled her into his arms, kissed her roughly.

'No one can ever come between us now, little one,' he told her on a strange, harsh note. He looked at her. 'Are there any more misunderstandings, I wonder, floating around in that indignant little mind of yours? Have you been nursing your wrath over anything else? If so, we'd better have it out right now.'

Maddie's eyes fell away. She hesitated.

'There is just one thing,' she admitted, 'although there's no question of wrath entering into this one!'

'We'll deal with it, then. What is it?'

'Kareena.' Steve swore softly as she said that name. 'It's just that I thought – well, what I mean is, I thought—'

'I can imagine what you thought, Madeleine,' Steve interrupted her ineffectual mutterings dryly. 'I worked out just what you must have thought – what you may even have been *led* to think – when I found out from Skeet's letter that you hadn't married after all. You'd simply run away. I went back over everything, trying to pick up some clues, and I remembered the look in your eyes, at the breakfast-table, that last morning at Bibbi. A sort of trapped look, it was, of pure desperation. You'd made up your mind to clear out that morning, hadn't you, Maddie? Am I right?'

She nodded silently.

'Sit down again, and I'll tell a little bit about Kareena.'

He put her back into her chair, took the cane one again, and began to fashion himself a cigarette. When he had done that, he stretched out his long legs, leaned back, and gave her a level regard.

'Kareena's what you might call an old family friend – the family's, rather than mine personally. Her uncle and my own father were very close mates all their days. They both had the same pastoral interests, and were active politically – a couple of tough old pioneers, you might call them. Kareena used to come up often to stay as a child, and so we saw a good deal of each other, I being the older by only a couple of years. When my parents and her uncle died, she seemed to want to keep coming, and I didn't try to stop her, because of the old associations. I sometimes do things like that for friendship's sake, Maddie, and I'm beginning to find out that it can land one in all sorts of bother!' He paused, grinned. 'Look where my friendship with Gerald Masterton landed me, for instance – in the role of the big bad wolf, my one desire to oust his lovely daughter out of her rightful inheritance and take his property to myself! Ah, well!' He pulled on his cigarette, exhaled, continued. 'Kareena has had an understanding that she doesn't need to wait to be asked up. I can't keep my eye on the social calendar, I've better things to do. Usually the phone just rings, and it's Kareena to say she'll be up for the polo, or the winter ball, or the spring meeting, or some such goddam' thing – I never really thought about it much. This last time, though, there was nothing on socially, nothing at all, and that rather puzzled me, for a start. I remember now that I had told her a bit about you when I took her out that time in Sydney – even then, I was a little bit in love with you, my darling, and it was a temptation to talk about you, I'm afraid. I know I didn't say much, beyond the fact that you were a rather lovely young girl, and that you'd be at Yattabilla for a year so that the place could become yours legally – you know the sort of thing. I thought nothing more about it.'

He looked about him for an ash-tray, reached for the cheap tin one on the table behind him. It had a beer advertisement running round the sides, and a boy at school had given it to Skeet last week.

'I didn't even connect that conversation with her recent visit to Bibbi – not until yesterday, when Skeet's letter arrived and I began to go over everything in my mind. I knew that I intended to fly down to Sydney right away, because I just had to find you, but I wanted to square Kareena first. I phoned her, and put a few questions to her. She beat about the bush for a while at first, but actually went so far as to admit that she had recognized you the moment she saw you in Noonday as the girl who walked past us in the nightclub one night. I'd already told her about taking you for a meal in the Blue Balcony, and then I let you walk straight past our table that night without a hint of recognition. To Kareena it could add up to only one thing, so she decided to stay on at Bibbi to do a spot of meddling, I suspect. She said a lot of things to me, then, Maddie, that I won't bother you with and would prefer to forget – accused me of hiding things, of a sneaking regard for you and so forth. I've no doubt that from the moment she had these suspicions, she started scheming to keep us apart. Poor Kareena!' He sighed. 'She was certainly livid when I told her on the phone that what I felt for you was much more than a sneaking regard, and that I was coming to Sydney to ask you to marry me! She hung up on me! I don't think Kareena will ever trouble us again, darling, because she knows she's rather overplayed her hand.'

Maddie smiled. 'But you *didn't*, Steve,' she murmured, dimpling.

'Didn't what?'

'Didn't ask me. To marry you, I mean.'

'My God, I don't believe I did!' Steve was out of his chair and across to hers, pulling her up into his arms again. He cradled her head against his chest. 'You will marry me, won't you, Maddie?' he said, into her hair. 'I want you for my wife, darling, quite desperately. Will you?'

'Of course I will. I mean, yes, *please*.'

He kissed her fiercely, as if he could never let her go, and Maddie felt herself melting against him in that divine state of ecstatic half-reality.

Steve put her from him with a groan.

'Let's make it soon, darling. There's nothing to wait for now, is there?' He sounded shaken, hoarse. 'Dear heaven, I'd never have lasted that year out, anyway!' He laced her fingers through his, looking at her with tenderness. 'We'll get a licence tomorrow, Maddie. We're going home to Bibbi as man and wife, do you hear?'

'Yes, Steve,' was her submissive reply.

The banging of the front door announced Skeet. He stood just inside the room, staring for one incredulous moment at the tanned, tall man who still held his sister in his arms. Then he threw down his schoolbag and hurled himself at them, whooping with sheer joy.

'Sh! Skeet, the landlady!' Maddie's warning was automatic.

'Crikey, Steve! It's *good* to see you! Crikey, it is!'

Steve mussed the ginger hair into spikes, smiling down at him.

'Did you get my letter, Steve, the one I wrote from school? Did you reckon it was a decent letter – well, I mean, fairly decent?' Skeet qualified modestly.

'I reckon it was *very* decent,' Steve assured him earnestly. 'In fact, Skeet, I'd go so far as to say it's the most welcome letter I've ever had in my whole life.'

'Dinkum, Steve?'

'Fair dinkum, feller,' was Steve's oddly serious reply. 'I'm going to keep that letter for the rest of my days.'

Skeet wrinkled his freckled nose.

'I'll have to tell the teacher. I didn't know it was as good as all *that*! Where's the tea, Maddie? Are we having some 'cos Steve's here, or do we still have to make things spin out?'

'Skeet!' She blushed, reproving him.

'Well, that's what you're always saying – and you've got the fire on full, too! Where on earth did you get the money, Mad?'

'*Skeet!*' she choked. 'I'll get the tea.'

Steve chucked Skeet softly under the chin.

'It's a special day, Skeet, that's why we're not waiting till later to eat those biscuits – if biscuits there are? We'll eat the whole lot now, and anything else that's around as well, and then you'll put on your best trousers, and your sister will put on her prettiest dress, and we'll all go out on the town. We'll have the biggest meal you ever ate in your life, because we're celebrating this very special day, all three of us!'

'What are we ceb – celebrating?' Skeet stumbled on the word.

When Steve told him, his eyes got round with wonder, and excitement brought vivid spots of colour to his cheeks.

'Gee! You mean, we'll be living at your place? At Bibbi?'

'That's right. When you're grown up you won't, of course. You'll be living at your own place instead, at Yattabilla, but it will be right next door. In the meantime, you'll live at Yattabilla, though, and Billy Sundown and I will show you how to do all the things you'll need to do some day for yourself on Yattabilla.'

'Crikey!' breathed Skeet. Then a thought struck him. '*She* won't be there, will she, at Bibbi? I don't think Maddie an' me will like it much if *she's* there.'

'She?'

'Kareena.' Skeet uttered the name with supreme disparagement.

Steve shook his head positively. 'There'll just be the three of us, Skeet, you and Maddie and me. And Mrs. Farrell, of course.'

'And Etta? Can't we have Etta?'

To our devoted Harlequin Readers:
Fill in handy coupon below and send off this page.

Harlequin Romances

TITLES STILL IN PRINT

- ☐ 51009 NURSE AT FAIRCHILDS, M. Norrell
- ☐ 51010 DOCTOR OF RESEARCH, E. Houghton
- ☐ 51011 THE TURQUOISE SEA, H. Wilde
- ☐ 51012 NO OTHER HAVEN, K. Blair
- ☐ 51013 MARY INTO MAIR, J. Ray
- ☐ 51014 HOUSE OF LORRAINE, R. Lindsay
- ☐ 51015 SWEET ARE THE WAYS, E. Summers
- ☐ 51016 TWO PATHS, J. Macleod
- ☐ 51017 ATTACHED TO DOCTOR MARCHMONT, J. Shore
- ☐ 51018 HOSPITAL IN THE TROPICS, G. Fullbrook
- ☐ 51019 FLOWER OF THE MORNING, C. Conway
- ☐ 51020 NO JUST CAUSE, S. Barrie
- ☐ 51021 FOLLY TO BE WISE, S. Seale
- ☐ 51022 YOUNG ELLIS, M. Hilton
- ☐ 51023 THE SWEET SURRENDER, R. Burghley
- ☐ 51024 THE HOUSE OF DISCONTENT, E. Wyndham
- ☐ 51925 SURGERY IN THE HILLS, I. Ferrari
- ☐ 51026 DOCTOR IN CORSICA, E. Gilzean
- ☐ 51027 THE LONELY SHORE, A. Weale
- ☐ 51028 THE MASTER OF NORMANHURST, M. Malcolm
- ☐ 51029 CHOOSE WHICH YOU WILL, M. Burchell
- ☐ 51030 THE BLACK BENEDICTS, A. Charles
- ☐ 51031 FLOWERING DESERT, E. Hoy
- ☐ 51032 BELOVED TYRANT, V. Winspear

∞∞∞∞∞∞∞∞∞∞∞∞∞∞∞∞∞∞∞

Harlequin Books, Dept. Z

Simon & Schuster, Inc., 11 West 39th St.
New York, N.Y. 10018

☐ Please send me information about Harlequin Romance Subscribers Club.

Send me titles checked above. I enclose .50 per copy plus .15 per book for postage and handling.

Name ....

Address ....

City .... State .... Zip ....

MAIL THIS COUPON TODAY

Steve's lips curled into an amused grin.

'I suppose we could have Etta, too,' he conceded. 'We'll bring her over from Yattabilla easily enough if you particularly want her, but there are lots of hens at Bibbi, if you remember, Skeet.'

'But will there be chicks?' Skeet asked anxiously.

'There are hens sitting on eggs right now – one or two of them at the very least,' Steve assured him, 'so you can count on chicks, too, I reckon.'

'But will they be the right sort of eggs? Will the hens know if they're the right sort of eggs, Steve? Etta didn't.' Skeet sounded worried.

'The Bibbi hens will.' Maddie heard Steve's deep voice, grave and unsmiling, as she placed the cups on the tray at the other end of the room. 'The Bibbi hens will know all right, you can take it from me. Bibbi knows what it's doing, and you'll find out all sorts of exciting things there, Skeet. It can teach you so much, because it's been there for so much longer than you or I – since the beginning of time itself, probably. Bibbi always knows just what it's doing. You needn't worry any more about anything, Skeet old feller, because Bibbi *always* knows!'